"To protect you I should step back." He rubbed his thumb along her bottom lip. **"But the idea of someone else being with you, touching you is more than I can tolerate."**

Her hand played with the scruff on the tip of his chin. "I wouldn't let anyone else touch me."

"What about me?"

"You can touch me as much as you want." She whispered the response because it felt right to let the words dance softly off her tongue.

After that his mouth dipped and his lips slipped over hers. Heat beat off her body and blood rushed to her head. Sensations walloped her—dizziness, elation. She craved his touch and wrapped her arms around her neck to pull him in closer.

Dear Harlequin Intrigue Reader,

For nearly thirty years fearless romance has fueled every Harlequin Intrigue book. Now we want everyone to know about the great crime stories our fantastic authors write and the variety of compelling miniseries we offer. We think our new cover look complements and enhances our promise to deliver edge-of-your-seat reads in all six of our titles—and brand-new titles every month!

This month's lineup is packed with nonstop mystery in *Smoky Ridge Curse,* the third in Paula Graves's Bitterwood P.D. trilogy, exciting action in *Sharpshooter,* the next installment in Cynthia Eden's Shadow Agents miniseries, and of course fearless romance—whether from newcomers Jana DeLeon and HelenKay Dimon or veteran author Aimée Thurlo, we've got every angle covered.

Next month buckle up as Debra Webb returns with a new Colby Agency series featuring The Specialists. And in November *USA TODAY* bestselling author B.J. Daniels takes us back to "The Canyon" for her special *Christmas at Cardwell Ranch* celebration.

Lots going on and lots more to come. Be sure to check out www.Harlequin.com for what's coming next.

Enjoy,

Denise Zaza

Senior Editor

Harlequin Intrigue

RUTHLESS

—

HelenKay Dimon

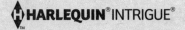

To my husband, James, for believing when
I was ready to give up hope.

Recycling programs
for this product may
not exist in your area.

ISBN-13: 978-0-373-69707-6

RUTHLESS

Copyright © 2013 by HelenKay Dimon

Printed in U.S.A.

www.Harlequin.com

ABOUT THE AUTHOR

Award-winning author HelenKay Dimon spent twelve years in the most unromantic career ever—divorce lawyer. After dedicating all that effort to helping people terminate relationships, she is thrilled to deal in happy endings and write romance novels for a living. Now her days are filled with gardening, writing, reading and spending time with her family in and around San Diego. HelenKay loves hearing from readers, so stop by her website, www.helenkaydimon.com, and say hello.

Books by HelenKay Dimon

CAST OF CHARACTERS

Pax Weeks—A former agent with the Defense Intelligence Agency and current member of the Corcoran Team. An on-the-job injury has him conducting "easy" surveillance at a coffee shop.

Kelsey Moore—She broke away from her scam-artist father to become an independent business owner. Her coffee shop means everything to her, but her family's activities put her in danger.

Bryce Kingston—He grew up the hard way on the rough streets of Baltimore to start a multimillion-dollar information and intelligence company. Having tasted the good life, he's not ready to let someone take it all away.

Glenn Harber—Bryce's promising assistant. He knows everything, has all the answers, but is there more to him than the boss thinks?

Dan Breckman—A consultant for Bryce's company. He's asking questions and appears to be an inside man. Question is: Whose man is he?

Sean Moore—Kelsey's brother had a promising career at Kingston, Inc. until privileged information went missing. Now everyone is pointing fingers at him.

Sanford Moore—Kelsey and Sean's scam-artist father. He pulled strings to get out of jail, but he's still on the lookout for a big score, even if it means sacrificing his kids to get it.

Connor Bowen—The leader of the Corcoran Team. He has some secrets of his own, but his loyalty to his team is absolute.

Chapter One

Kelsey Moore balanced a tray of croissants and gooey pastries on one arm and counted how many she had left for the end-of-the-morning rush. Ten in the morning was too early to break out the sandwich menu, which meant she had to make the breakfast offerings last for another hour. Hard to do if another round of the fanny pack and matching T-shirt crowd descended.

Not that she was complaining. The summer season had finally hit full swing in Annapolis, Maryland, as the increased number of buses and lack of on-street parking spaces showed. Tourists poured in to visit the quaint shops, check out that Naval Academy a few blocks over and wander down to the City Dock, also known as Ego Alley thanks to the expensive yachts that pulled up there.

Her coffee shop, Decadent Brew, sat in a prime location on Main Street, midway between the waterfront and the Maryland State House. She'd love to take credit for having the foresight to buy the two-story slim town house, but that honor went to her aunt, who ran it as a coffee and knitting shop for years.

Kelsey dropped the yarn part when she inherited it because she could barely sew on a button let alone figure out how to knit or purl. She had added a lunch menu, local art to walls, bookcases and sofas. In a rough economy, the small changes allowed her to survive and build a loyal following over the coffee chains. Not thrive, but pay the bills...usually.

Using tongs, she loaded up the display case with the last two doughnuts and the rest of the chocolate croissants. About half the tables were full, many with patrons more intent on typing on their laptops than actually eating anything. Still, silverware clanked, and the low rumble of conversation mixed with the piped-in music.

The steady beat and cheerful mood suited her. She liked to be busy, liked to see the seats filled, but never lost focus. After two years in business she knew how to keep one eye on the college kid making the lattes—this year his name was Mike—and the other on Lindy, the cute new high school senior who spent more time flirting and tugging on her short skirt than cleaning off the tables.

If Kelsey had a third eye she'd keep it locked on the front door because it was time. *He* came around this time every day, or he had for the past two weeks.

He'd walk in, his gaze searching for her. The corner of his mouth would lift in that breath-stealing smile and her stomach would do the stupid bouncing thing that made her feel younger than Lindy. Certainly more like fifteen than twenty-six, which she was.

As if thinking about him could conjure him up, the bell above the door chimed. Kelsey glanced up to see him holding the door for a family heading outside. He stood a bit over six feet with the kind of broad shoulders that made women look and then turn and look again. Dirty blond hair and eyes she knew from past encounters edged the border between brown and green.

Between the faded jeans and the trim gray T-shirt, she could easily call up a mental image of his bare stomach without ever having seen it. Something she'd done a little more often than she wanted to admit.

He nodded a welcome to a table of sixty-something women, who rotated between staring at him and whispering to each other. But he saved the wave and that killer smile for Kelsey.

Her hand tightened on the tray to keep from dropping it. "Hey there."

"Good morning," he said when he stopped across the counter from her.

"So far. How are you?"

The couple off to his left ran through the exact makeup of a caramel macchiato with Mike, which gave her an extra minute with Paxton. An unusual name but she'd remember his even if it were something easily forgettable, like Bob. A long line a few days ago gave her the excuse to ask his name. Owning the place did have its benefits.

"Not to scare you, but there's one of those walking tours a few blocks away and headed in this direction."

She enjoyed the flirting, but she didn't ignore business. "Let's hope they're thirsty."

"In that case I'm happy I'm here first, before it's standing room only in here." He leaned against the counter, because that's what he always did.

The combination of the slight limp and short hair made her think military, possibly returning from an overseas tour. Living in a navy area tended to take a person's mind in that direction. Still, he had the muscular build, complete with bulging biceps and a vine tattoo peeking out from under his sleeve. Military or not, it amounted to a pretty lethal punch to her usual common-sense theory of not mixing business with pleasure.

She tried to think of something clever to say. When nothing came to her, she winced over her complete lack of smoothness and set the tray down. "You want the usual?"

He pointed at the display case. "Add in whatever you have extra of or might have trouble selling today."

As if she didn't already have a crush on the guy.

She went to the tap at the coffee-of-the-day dispenser as the bell above the door dinged again. One look around the counter and she realized she'd need a trip to the stockroom because there was only one to-go cup left after the one for Paxton.

A group of kids came in, all shouting as their gazes stayed fixed on their phones. She turned to face the front of the store again to send a quiet-down gaze and spied the two guys hovering behind the noisy kids.

Black suits, dark scowls and a laserlike focus on…well, her. She immediately thought *politicians,* but the Maryland General Assembly wasn't in session. That left lawyers or government types. Either way, something about their intensity had her squirming.

Paxton cleared his throat. "You okay?"

Her gaze went back to him. She read concern in his narrowed eyes, heard it in the sudden roughness of his deep voice, and forced a smile to her lips. She hoped it rose to the level of sunny. "Absolutely."

She snapped the lid on his coffee and snuck a few more peeks at the suited patrons while she scrambled to get Paxton a bear claw. She pretended not to notice as the suit-wearers closed in a step at a time, never saying a word to each other and not bothering to look at the menu board over her head.

She put the plate down on the counter harder than expected in front of Paxton. The smack of ceramic against glass had both Mike and Paxton staring at her. Before she could babble out some excuse, Paxton put a hand over hers. Warmth seeped into her skin.

"Maybe you should sit down."

"I'm fine." And by that she meant spooked. The two guys

hadn't done or said anything, yet their presence had her swallowing and shifting her weight around.

"We could go out front for second."

"Really. It's okay." She said the words because she wanted the men out, and the only way to have that was to wait on them. They now stood right behind Paxton's impressive shoulder, and for some reason she wanted them away from him, too.

Still, he hesitated. He balanced his coffee and his wallet. "If you're sure."

"Absolutely. And today is on me." She pushed the plate closer. Before Paxton could argue, she glanced at her unwanted guests. "What can I get the two of you?"

For a second they held on to their silence. Finally, the taller one on the left blinked. "Black coffee to go."

"Two?" When he frowned at her, she tried again. "I mean, do you each want one?"

Paxton held his position at the counter, and the men didn't try to shove around him. They didn't look at him, either, but he stared at them as if he had them under some sort of visual scan.

"One cup only," the taller man said.

Unusual but not scary. She repeated that mantra as she turned back to the coffeepot and the blank space where the last cup sat a second ago. Another look and she watched Mike top off a latte with foam in the cup she wanted.

She could send him on a restocking run, but with the way her chest tightened she suddenly needed to gulp in as much air as possible. Better to do that away from the patrons. She held up a finger. "I'll be back in one second."

Before the men could argue, she took off. She shuffled around and pushed open the door to the narrow hall behind the main dining area marked Private. She kept moving as she passed the door to her office on the right and the stock-room on the left and finally hit the back entry.

Two slams against the safety bar and she had it open. The humid air rolled in, giving her the sensation of standing in front of a low-watt hair dryer.

With her eyes closed she counted to ten and tried to calm her overreaction. This is what happened to her now. Ever since her brother stopped communicating, her mind played vivid and scary games with the benign truth around her. Last night a guy stood on the sidewalk outside her upstairs apartment too long and she immediately assumed he was casing the place. It was as if her life had become a strange action movie.

When she reached ten in her silent countdown, she let out one final dramatic breath. Time to get back to work.

Fearing the air-conditioning would never stop running and her electric bill would soar if she kept the door open, she yanked on it, hearing it creak and moan as she tried to slam it shut. The thing weighed a ton, but she wrestled it closed every single day. Not that she had a choice now. Another min-ute away from the counter and Mike might sit down with his own laptop and play on the internet instead of work.

She smiled at the idea as she glanced over her shoulder toward the front of the shop. At the end of the hall stood one of the tall unwanted visitors. Seeing him there, in the small space between her and the freedom of the front room wiped out any amusement she'd felt.

She forgot about locking the door and turned to face the unwanted stranger. She said the first thing—the only thing—that popped into her mind. "You can't be here."

He closed the distance between them in a few steps. If he reached out he could touch her, but his hands remained at his back. "We'll be leaving by the door behind you."

We? Yeah, no way. "Wrong."

"I'm not playing." His arm dropped to his side.

She blinked at the gun in his hand and a paralyzing fear streaked through her nerves. "I'll scream."

"And put everyone out front in danger? I don't think so."

She turned to race out the back door and it burst open, bouncing with a crash and pinning her against the hallway wall. Unwanted visitor number two filled the entrance. She opened her mouth to let out the scream rumbling around in her chest when the man behind her grabbed her and clamped a hand over her mouth.

She kicked and threw her elbows. Even tried bending forward in the hope of breaking the guy's hold.

He snapped her back into him, almost lifting her off the floor. "One word and we shoot everyone in the shop."

When the attacker's hot breath blew over her cheek, she choked back the bile rising in her throat. Her mind raced as she mentally flipped through her options for saving herself and everyone in her shop.

Yell, run, fight. The most important thing was to not let these guys drag her away. She knew that much from the safety class she'd taken through the police station. But she had to get somewhere other than a claustrophobic back hallway.

To stall, she nodded. Instead of easing, the attacker's arm wrapped tighter against her neck. Muscle pressed against her windpipe. She clawed against his forearm in a futile attempt to keep him from crushing out her air supply.

The taller one pointed at the back door. "Let's get her out of here before that kid realizes she's gone and tries to play hero."

Mike.

Paxton.

Her brain flashed to images of all of them. To all the innocent people on the other side of the wall. Then her attackers started moving. She dragged her feet and grabbed for a hold in the chipped wall. Fingernails scraped against old paint, but she couldn't halt his progress.

Inhaling deep and gathering all her strength, she lifted her foot and nailed her attacker in the shin. At the thud of heel on bone, they slammed to a stop. The guy swore as he threw her body against the wall and held her there with his weight against her back.

Her head hit plaster and the world around her tilted. She gasped, trying to drag enough air into her lungs and brain to keep thinking.

The crunch of her nose against the wall sent pain spiraling through her. She turned her head and blinked when the crushing ache of her cheek against the wall threatened to be too much. Her body felt as if it were being ripped apart and smashed into a small ball at the same time.

In the next second, all the pressure vanished. The sudden change had her dazed and sliding to the floor. As her body fell, she saw a flash of gray.

Limp seemingly gone, Paxton moved in a blur. His body honed and aimed like a weapon, he came in the back door fighting. He jammed an elbow into the smaller attacker's head and knocked him into the wall. The guy went down in a motionless whoosh.

Something whizzed in front of her. She glanced over and saw Paxton standing with his arm out and his furious glare aimed at the taller attacker. She followed the line of Paxton's body and watched the other attacker scramble, his shoes scuffing against the floor, before he dropped. A red blotch spread on his stomach a second later as his gun dropped and spun across the floor.

Her first look at the knife was of the way it stuck out of the attacker's body. Even with his eyes closed and his body slumped to the side, he scared the crap out of her.

It all happened so fast and with less sound than if she had been moving boxes around back there. The pulsing tension seeped out of the hallway, but she couldn't take it all in. Sounds muffled, but she thought she heard someone talking. With her head tilted back, she saw Paxton grab the abandoned gun and point it at the bleeding man before hitting him with the end of it.

Paxton was talking but not looking at her. The words refused to come together in her brain. Finally, he glanced down at her, and the scowl marking his forehead eased. He dropped down to balance on the balls of his feet and winced as he went. The move put them face-to-face.

"Are you okay?" he asked.

The calm words brushed against her and she answered with the truth. "No."

His gaze traveled all over her. "Were you hit?"

"I don't think so." She closed her eyes to keep the room from spinning, but the reality of where she was had them popping open again. She tried to sit up, hoping her legs would hold her if she somehow wrestled her fatigued body to her feet. "My employees and the people—"

He put his hand on her noninjured knee, and the light touch held her down. "Everyone is fine. They don't even know anything happened back here."

The noise. The slamming doors. The grunts and yelling. None of that fit together with his assurance. "How is that possible?"

"I need a team and possibly medical." He talked to the air.

He kept issuing orders. Something about identities and watching the front. She really focused on him then, letting her gaze wander over the firm chin and across his broad chest. Apparently he threw knives. He had the attacker's gun plus another one.

In a matter of minutes he'd morphed from cute flirty guy with an injury to scary fighter guy.

"Is the limp real?" She blurted out the question before she could stop it.

"Yes." He touched his ear. "Now, Joel."

"Joel?"

Then she saw it. A tiny piece of silver. He had a microphone and was talking to someone who wasn't actually in the hallway.

Her eyes closed as a wave of nausea rolled over her. She hadn't dreamed any of it, and all of her fears of walking into the middle of a terrifying gun battle had come true.

That left one very big question.

She opened her eyes and stared at him again. "Who are you really?"

"Same guy you served the coffee to."

She tried to scoff but she didn't have the energy or extra breath. "I don't think so."

"You should probably call me Pax." He had the nerve to smile at her as he stood up.

This time she didn't buy the full mouth or twinkle in his eyes. "You're not a normal coffee customer."

"I am, but I'm also something else."

Dread spilled into her stomach. "What?"

"Your informal bodyguard."

Chapter Two

From the huge brown eyes to the grim line of her mouth, Kelsey looked about two seconds away from striking out. Maybe screaming her head off. Both options sounded bad to Pax. He wasn't a fan of throwing up, either, and the sudden green taint to her skin suggested that was a real possibility.

He reached down to help her up, but she shrank back against the wall, her petite frame curling in on itself. In the tucked position, her long hair fell over her shoulders, shielding her face from view and hiding the ripped strap holding her shirt on her shoulder. The denim shorts showed off her lean legs and a red welt right above her knee.

Seeing her injured and scared dropped a black curtain of rage over him. Every cell inside him craved revenge. He seriously considered removing his knife and then plunging it into the bad guy a second time.

But attack mode would have to wait. They had to get out of there, which meant providing a dose of comfort and reassurance. Not two of his strengths, sure, but since joining up with the Corcoran Team he'd been polishing the skills.

These jobs weren't like the ones he'd worked at his old employer, the Defense Intelligence Agency. There, he'd tracked down military intelligence leaks. He dealt in bad guys, dangerous situations and threats to service members.

In his new life he still went after bad guys, but now his

main objective centered on rescuing kidnapping victims. Or even better, stopping kidnapping threats before they happened, something he'd basically failed to do with Kelsey.

"Kelsey, it's going to be okay." Pitching his voice low and keeping it as soothing as possible, he said the words even though he knew she was in no condition to hear them.

She glanced at the body on the floor just a few feet away from her thigh and then back to Pax. "How can you say that? Look around you."

He wasn't sure what to say or how much to share about his real reason for visiting her shop almost every day for weeks, so he tried to evade. "Admittedly, the attack was a surprise."

Her eyes narrowed as fire sparked behind them. She added to the angry-warrior-woman stance by brushing her hair off her shoulder and staring him down. "That's your response?"

So much for thinking she was scared.

She shook her head. "You pretend to be injured—"

"I actually am injured. Well, was."

"—and you storm in here."

"By that you mean walked in the front door and ordered coffee, though from your comment I would guess my limp wasn't as well hidden as I thought." And didn't that tick him off.

The cracking sound came the second after she clenched her jaw. "You flew across the hallway a second ago, so stop pretending you're hurt and tell me who you really are."

"Maybe we could agree on the term *recovering*."

She blew out a long breath as her shoulders slumped. "Are you trying to be annoying?"

In light of her response, Pax wasn't sure how he should play this. "My brother would tell you that comes naturally. I don't have to try very hard at it."

He'd hoped to take her mind off the death choking the air around them by keeping the mood light. Seeing her pressed against the wall a few minutes ago started his mind unraveling. He'd assumed he'd clean up the mess and she'd be grateful. Maybe do the terrified thing and shake and cry, possibly need some consoling.

That was a normal reaction. This was not. She came out swinging. He half expected her to fight off his attempts at calming the situation and punch him in the groin.

Tension continued to zing around the enclosed space. Guns down and his knife still in use in the unidentified man's stomach, and yet Pax couldn't let his guard ease. Not when the woman in front of him vibrated with unspent energy and seemed determined to question everything he said.

She didn't even blink. "So now you have a brother?"

"Technically I've always had one since he's older." When the mumble of conversation from the front of the shop seeped through the walls and someone banged on the door to this back area asking why it was locked, Pax talked louder to drag her attention back to him. "His name is Davis."

She waved the comment off. Came very close to knocking against him while she moved her hands around. "I don't understand who you are or what's going on. And who are these two guys and why did they try to drag me outside?"

Pax surveyed the carnage. He had to move her off the property before these guys' friends missed them and came looking for trouble. "All good questions."

"Care to answer one?"

"Once we're out of here." Pax tapped the mic in his ear. "Ben? Finish clearing the shop and close the place down. Blame a gas leak and then get a medic because we have two down. Joel, I need you back here. Now."

Her sneakers scraped against the rough floor as she bent her knees and brought her feet closer to her butt. "Really?"

Pax wasn't clear which word led to the reaction. "What?"

"You're really doing some sort of spy-act thing in the middle of all this?"

He despised that word. The way Hollywood portrayed undercover agents and people in law enforcement as if they all used shoe phones and exploding pens was ridiculous. "It's possible you watch too much television."

She sat up even straighter, her shoulders coming off the wall and her hands falling to the floor on each side of her hips. "Okay, Mr. Good Samaritan. How about calling the police...and what do you mean by medic? Call an ambulance. I have customers and employees out front and need to know they're safe."

From the clear eyes and stronger voice he guessed she'd found her emotional and physical footing. That likely spelled trouble for him.

"Then there's the mess back here. That one will wake up eventually." She pointed at the downed man closest to the back door. "And that one is losing blood thanks to your knife skills."

Pax hoped she didn't expect an apology. "Yeah."

"He's not dead, is he?

"Unfortunately, no. Unconscious and bleeding." Pax glanced at the other man. "And that one is lucky not to be bleeding. I'm thinking about stabbing him just because."

She swallowed and made a face that suggested she didn't like whatever she'd tasted. "In a few seconds I'll have to go over there and try to help the bloody one, and the idea of touching him after...well, it makes me want to throw up and kind of furious at you."

Yeah, she'd definitely moved from scared—and that had been pretty fleeting—to ticked off. As the clear target of whatever thoughts bounced around in her head and put that scowl on her face, he dropped the lighter tone. It wasn't working anyway. Didn't take a fancy shoe phone to figure that one out.

He held up his hand in a gesture he hoped telegraphed peace and maybe a touch of surrender. "Everything will be handled, but not in the way you're suggesting."

Then it started. She slid her hands closer to her body and shifted in a move so slight he almost missed it. He guessed she intended to struggle to her feet and then make a run for it. He was ready for the bolt. He just wished they could short-cut the disbelief and go right to the part where she got in the car and let him take her to safety.

Not that he deserved that level of trust from her. They barely knew each other. Sure, they'd flirted and he'd benefit-ted in the form of free bear claws now and then, but dough-nuts didn't change the facts. He was there to watch over her, to see if her missing brother made contact.

It was supposed to be a simple surveillance op, since that's all anyone at the Corcoran Team thought he could handle post-shooting incident. Little did they know the supposed "easy" job would lead to a backroom shoot-out.

"Don't even think about it." When she frowned at him, he filled her in. "Whatever big exit plan is in your head? Forget it. You're not getting by me. We need to get you somewhere safe, and then we can talk all of this through."

"We?"

"I think he's referring to me." Joel stepped over the man at the back door and moved inside. He hitched his thumb over his shoulder toward the alley outside. "Car's waiting."

Pax reached down a second time to get her off the floor. "Come on, Kelsey."

Her gaze bounced from him to Joel and back again as she crowded closer to the wall. "No way."

"These guys on the floor could have partners," Joel said.

Pax welcomed Joel's verbal assist but could do without the smirk. "I can guarantee that's true."

"Why should I trust you? I don't know you." She peeked around Pax's legs at Joel. "Or him."

When she drew in a deep breath, Pax dropped to his haunches again and bit down on his lip to keep from yelling. Ignoring the shot of pain, he held a hand over her mouth, careful not to get his palm too close to those teeth.

"Don't do that." She mumbled something against his hand but he ignored it and kept lecturing. "I know you want to yell for help but screaming could bring more attackers. Do you want that?"

She took several breaths before she shook her head.

Pax inhaled long and deep, trying to see this from her perspective and keep his anger in check. With her family history it was no wonder she went with wariness over fear. He knew only the scraps in her brother's file about a deceased mother, but the background of Kelsey's criminal father wasn't a mystery. His name had seen a lot of time in the papers a few years back. The truth, whatever really went on in this family, could be much worse.

"You see me every day," Pax pointed out as he stood up again. This time it took longer and more energy. Too many more deep knee bends and he'd crash to the floor.

"As a customer only."

Joel chuckled. "And she lands a verbal blow. I bet that hurt."

"You're not helping," Pax said under his breath and included a string of profanity to make his point.

Last thing he needed was a real-time reminder of just how attracted he was to Kelsey and how it suddenly seemed to run in only one direction. Especially since she was scowling at him, looking as if she might be planning his funeral.

"Joel, is it?" She shifted her weight and slid her body up

the wall. When her knees wobbled, she reached out for Pax, grabbing on to his forearm and steadying her balance again. Her hand dropped a second later.

"Joel Kidd. Yes, ma'am." The corner of Joel's mouth kicked up in a smile when she talked to him.

"Call the police."

The smile fumbled. "I'm afraid I can't—"

"Do that. Yeah, I get it." She stepped away from the wall and inched closer to the far end of the hallway. "Paxton...or whatever his name is, said the same thing."

"My name really is Paxton. I just prefer Pax."

But she'd stopped listening. She glanced around the floor and took a wide jump over the bleeding attacker's body. "I'm going to go out front and check on Mike. I might even scream if it looks like it's clear and you're the problem instead of the solution."

Pax grabbed her arm in time. He had her spinning around and standing only a few inches in front of him. At six feet he loomed over her by a good six inches. All those years playing football and the genes from a father he never knew had gifted Pax with broad shoulders.

His size tended to intimidate people. Using the factor to get his way never bothered him before. If it meant saving her, it wouldn't bother him now, either.

"No." Enough talk. He started walking toward the back door, taking her with him. He didn't squeeze or pull, but with his elbow tucked and her body swept in close to his, he had the balance advantage and moving her didn't take much pressure against her skin.

"Excuse me?"

He kept the lock on her elbow. "I tried this the nice way."

"When?"

They blew by Joel, who had dropped to the floor to check the pockets of both fallen attackers. "Uh, Pax."

The tone signaled caution as much as if Joel had thrown up a flashing red light. Pax shortened his stride and stopped a few steps from the back door.

"We are going to walk out there and get into the SUV." He lowered his voice, forcing the tension to leave his jaw before it cracked from the pressure. "We are going to get out of here and to somewhere safe. Then we can talk all of this out. But, Kelsey—and you need to understand this—we are leaving. No discussion."

The muscles in her arm went slack. All of a sudden it was easy to glide her across the floor and direct her where he wanted her to go. Pax knew that was a very bad sign.

This lady had the moves down cold—force your body to relax, and the person holding you will ease the grasp. Pax knew because he taught self-defense classes at the YMCA and had advised more than one class of women to avoid ever getting into a car with an attacker.

As the realization hit him, her body jerked. She slammed to a halt and pivoted away from him as she whipped her arm up, shrugging out of his hold. When he reached for her again, she ducked under the arc of his swing. Doubled over and head down in determination, she sprinted.

With his messed-up leg, she could have vaulted and took off and left him sputtering, but her sneaker snagged on the foot of the guy on the ground and she tripped. Her momentum took her flying and stumbling. She crashed against the wall next to the back door and stopped.

He swooped in before she could take off again. "Whoa."

He trapped her against the wall with his body, ignoring the uneasy sensation rumbling through him from mimicking the actions of the man who had attacked her earlier. Pax slapped his palms against the uneven cement on each side of her head and rested his body against hers, careful to crowd her but not smash into her.

She clearly saw it differently because the second his body touched against hers, she whipped into a wild frenzy. "Not again."

She kicked out behind her and raked her fingernails against the back of his hand. With her head shaking and shifting, she struggled and grunted. Energy pounded off her as every limb, every muscle, moved in concert against him.

This time, he threw his weight into the hold. He pressed his chest against her back and grabbed her wrists and stretched her arms out to keep them from flailing. Their heavy breathing mixed together as air pounded in his lungs. Beneath him, he could feel the rise and fall of her upper body on rough gasps.

She turned her head to the side and stared at Joel. Until that moment, Pax had forgotten his partner was even there. So much for calling in reinforcements. He could only hope Ben was having an easier time with the crowd out front.

"You could help me," she said to Joel.

"If it's any consolation, I plan on telling everyone back at the office about how close you came to getting the jump on Pax."

Pax swore under his breath. As if the shot to the thigh wasn't enough cause for ribbing. Now he'd have to hear about this. "Kelsey, listen to me."

"Why should I?" The harsh words lost their impact under the weak thread of her voice.

"You're in danger."

She turned her head and balanced her forehead against the wall. The position cut off all potential of eye contact with Pax and Joel. "Obviously."

"Not from me."

"You're the one who threw the knife. The same guy who's holding me now." She shrugged. "You're hurting me, by the way."

He eased his stance, shifting his weight to his heels and thinking to move away. Then he stopped. In addition to the sweet face and impressive legs, she was smart and skilled. He wouldn't put it past her to use guilt to break free.

He tried logic one last time. "There are men after you."

"Why?"

Pax glanced at Joel. The slight shake of his head mirrored Pax's feelings on the subject. It was too early and they had too little information on Kelsey to dump the truth on her. They needed to press her for information on her brother. But not here. Certainly not now.

Joel cleared his throat. "That's what we're here to figure out."

"And you two just happened to show up—"

"Three," Pax said.

"What?"

He didn't see a reason to hide the team. "Ben's out front."

"How comforting." She wiggled and pushed until he let her turn around. Anger and confusion battled in her eyes. "You understand why I'm confused. You guys all conveniently show up, claiming to be the good guys."

Pax knew he'd never used those words. "I get it."

"And?"

She deserved points for good questions and intelligence. The instructor side of him would pass her without trouble. In real life, her discomfort meant danger. And facing him, she had a clear shot at using the first attack move he taught women to use against men, and he had no intention of falling to his knees in pain.

That meant the conversation was over and he would end it. Right now.

"We're done with this." Her breath hiccuped and the sharp intake echoed in his ears as he bent over and lifted her off the ground. She landed on his shoulder with her head at his back. "Let's go."

Joel shook his head. "Man, this is a bad solution."

"It's the only one I have."

Kelsey stammered and spoke in half sentences. She finally got out a string of words. "What are you doing?"

"Since you want to do this the hard way, we will."

Then he walked out the back door as she started to scream.

Chapter Three

Kelsey stopped kicking and squirming as her brain rebooted. She looked down and saw his jeans and back, an odd from-above shot of his butt and the ground racing by beneath his feet. Being upside down with his fat-free shoulder digging into her stomach, she didn't have a good angle to nail him in the back. That was okay. She needed to save her energy and come up with a plan to get off this guy and out of there.

She also had to beat back the wave of disappointment swamping her. The wounded military hero backstory she'd created in her mind and spun into interesting tales didn't fit the real man at all. She'd secretly declared him a hottie and thought about him far too often once the workday ended and she lay in her bed.

Now she knew she'd picked the wrong description. Something that summed up a bossy, manhandling secretive liar would have been more appropriate.

Paxton or Pax or whatever he wanted to call himself carried weapons and got all grumbly and demanding when he wanted something. The idea she'd once thought of him as sweet and had piled all those free doughnuts on him…she wanted every delicious calorie back. The least he could have done was gain weight because really, she needed something to slow him down.

Even with the slight limp—an injury she now totally

viewed as an act—he'd stalked down the alley with only the barest crunch of gravel beneath his shoes to give away his position. The bouncing steps continued as they rounded the car and walked within a few feet of the SUV's back door.

Once he got her in there, breaking free could be impossible. No way was she going anywhere with two men she didn't know. She'd taken the lessons and listened to the lectures. She'd already lived through an attack once in her life, years ago.

She would not be a victim again.

She'd be smart, pick the exact right moment and then run in the direction of the nearest person or telephone, screaming her head off as she went.

The door on the opposite side of the car opened. Twisting around on Pax's shoulder, she looked through the window and spied Joel sliding across the passenger side of the backseat. She could only guess he was her assigned babysitter for their ride to wherever.

Just as she saw the gun in his hand, her butt smacked against the side of the car as Pax balanced her weight. Keys jangled and the world spun around her, the clear blue sky whizzing by, as her feet finally hit the ground.

Pax kept a steady hand on her arm as he reached for the door handle. "We're done with the nonsense, right?"

Whatever that meant. She nodded, trying to look obedient and terrified, though that last one wasn't much of a stretch for her limited acting skills. If the blood pounding in her ears and wild flip-flopping of her stomach were any indication, she registered pretty high on the terror scale.

He ducked his head and stared straight into her eyes. "Kelsey?"

"Fine, yes." She just needed him to shift an inch or two to the side, move a little out of the way, and she was out of there.

With a click, the door opened. He pulled it toward him

with slow precision, coaxing her into the small space he created. Inch by inch she crept closer to being penned in and vulnerable.

No way was this happening a second time. The first scarred her, left her sleep tortured and her trust in tatters for years. The seventeen-year-old version of her made a vow never to go back to that dark place, to fight no matter what, and she intended to honor that promise.

Angling her body, she turned to get a better position and set her weight so she could spring off her back leg and race down the alley to the open street beyond. She launched and miscalculated the opening. Her hip banged off the edge of the door.

Red lights danced in front of her eyes and her leg went numb. Then the pain came roaring on, pulsing and knee-buckling in its intensity. Her mouth dropped open to yelp but no sound escaped.

He threw the door open wide and put his hands on the sides of her waist in a gentle touch that somehow managed to hold her upright. Concern showed in his narrowed eyes. "Are you okay?"

"That hurt like a—"

"I bet."

He touched his fingers against the throbbing spot on the side of her leg. The rubbing eased the burning enough for her concentration to rev up again. She pushed out all sense of comfort and lowered her head, getting him to look down.

With her hands on his arm, she shoved with all her strength and bolted. She heard him swear as his body thudded against the side of the car. But she was gone. She sprinted down the alley, glancing around for any sign of life or a place to duck and hide. The wind whipped around her as footsteps thudded behind her, growing louder with each step.

"Kelsey, stop!" Pax's husky voice, fueled with fury, bounced off the brick walls, magnifying the sound.

She saw the bright light at the far end of the alley and headed for it. Thirty feet away, half the distance between the SUV and freedom, a shadow moved in. She opened her mouth to scream for help as she heard the skid of stones and felt a muscled arm band around her waist. The smell she associated with Pax—a mix of citrus and pine—fell over her.

She tried to wrestle away from him until she saw the familiar black suit on the stranger at the end of the alley. And the gun he held in his hand.

"Get down." The heat of Pax's body enveloped her the second before his words sank in.

The air rushed out of her and her footing failed. Pax's legs tangled with hers as his body wrapped around hers from behind. His weight pummeled into her and they both dropped through the air. She raised her hands and closed her eyes, waiting for her face to smack against the hard pavement and hoping her fingers could somehow minimize the painful blow.

Noise thundered around her until she couldn't tell the sounds of her screaming from the other shouts filling the air. Her legs took flight behind her. One minute she saw the ground racing up and the next they twisted and she landed with a hard smack against Pax's chest. He grunted and swore as his hand curled around her head and his body absorbed most of the impact.

They'd barely landed when he rolled and tucked her under him. In a continuous move, he came up over top of her and swung out his arm. One, two bangs boomed above her. She smelled a faint scent of burning and heard people yelling at the end of the alley for someone to call 911.

Pax's hand dropped and his body grew limp, pressing deeper against her. "Got him," he whispered.

In her head the whole scene took an hour, but she guessed it was less than a minute in real time. She let her head drop against the ground as she watched a puff of white cloud shift as it skimmed the blue sky. It took another second for her breathing to return to normal and her heart to stop knocking against the inside wall of her chest.

Her head fell to the side and she glanced back at the SUV. Joel lay stretched out on the seat with his hands still fixed on the gun with the weapon aimed. That fast, she remembered the suited man, and her gaze flipped back to the opening to the street where people now gathered. A man was down with a gun visible by his hand.

When she looked up again, Pax loomed over her, staring down. "I had to."

She tried to raise her hand and put her palm against his cheek, but her arms suddenly weighed a ton each. "You shot him."

Pax winced as if she'd struck him. "He was going for you."

She didn't understand the look of pain in his eyes. Who he really was and why he'd walked into her life were still parts of a greater mystery, but this time she didn't doubt his protection.

Maybe it was intuition or adrenaline, or just the shock of so much violence on the quaint streets of Annapolis. "Right."

His eyes narrowed as he struggled to sit up and help her do the same. "This is about your brother."

"I…wait, what?" Of all the things she expected him to say, that wasn't even on the list. "What are you talking about?"

"Your brother ticked off the wrong people and now someone wants to bring you in to flush Sean out."

The words pelted her. They scrambled and unscrambled, but she couldn't put them together in any logical way in her brain.

"Talk later. We need to get out of here." A shadow fell

over them. Joel bent over with his hands on his knees. His voice wobbled a bit on each word. "Ben's handling things out front, but the police are coming and we need to be gone."

She nodded because she had no idea what to say. This, like so much in her life, was about the men in it. First her dad, now Sean. Their choices. Their actions.

Pax grimaced as he stood up and stretched his legs. When he reached down to her, this time she grabbed his hand and jumped to her feet. Standing in front of him, her fingers speared through his, an odd calm blanketed her. They weren't out of danger and none of what had happened made sense, but for the first time since Pax walked through her door this morning, a sense of safety radiated through her.

He gave her hand a squeeze. "No more running."

"I don't trust you, but I'm not stupid. You always go with the guy who saved your life."

"Smart woman."

But she wasn't ready to turn to mush and follow every order he threw out. "I want answers."

"Then get in the car."

BRYCE KINGSTON BALANCED his palms against the sill and looked out his office window. His fingers tapped against the glass as he watched the steady lines of traffic move in each direction and with amazing slowness on the highway sixteen floors below.

After a quick glance at his watch, he shook his head with a harsh laugh. Never mind the hour of the day, barely lunchtime and nowhere near rush hour. The close-in proximity of Tysons Corner, Virginia, to Washington, D.C., meant cars idled and passengers baked in the burning sun and claustrophobic humidity as they tried to go anywhere in the summer heat.

The high-rise space, with its soaring windows and plush carpet, telegraphed the business image he wanted. The gran-

ite lobby and bank of security monitors, all designed by him
with a team of high-priced architects, created the desired pub-
lic impression of safety and wealth. He didn't have a fancy
water view or the prime location near the Kennedy Center,
but he had the end of the cul-de-sac spot in a business park
within a reasonable drive of the airport.

Then there was the real-estate advantage in terms of the
clients, and that's all that mattered to him as the founder of
Kingston Inc. One division provided high-speed communication services to the government, ensuring continuous service and functioning networks.

But the new division would be the key to the company's
future. He was sure of it. The high-tech division dealt with
top-secret electronic surveillance and assisted the intelligence community and military in collecting and relaying
information.

Not bad for a guy who spent most of his youth getting
beat up on the school bus for spending so much time in computer class.

After a few years of leaner times and financial insecurities, the business plan was back on track. Well, not all of it.
Sean Moore proved to be a wild card. Bryce never expected
a low-level computer programmer to sit at the heart of potential corporate-ruining disaster.

"Sir?" Bryce's assistant, Glenn Harber, stuck his head in
the small space he made when he opened the door.

Bryce didn't hear the knock, but he knew Glenn didn't
skip that requirement. Tall and lean and still an expert rower
and member of a team of young businessmen who met on
the Potomac River well before dawn twice per week, Glenn
knew about structure. He was not a man who shortcut the
rules or invaded privacy without a care.

Four years out of business school and loaded down with
two master's degrees and a host of other useless academic

information, Glenn had demonstrated his commitment to the company. He came in early and left late. He often flew on the corporate jet for meetings and visits to military bases for demonstrations. And right now he looked as if he'd eaten a heaping plate of rotten conference food.

"Come in." Bryce pushed away from the window and sat down in his overstuffed desk chair.

The wife had chosen the décor. To Bryce, the dark furniture, set off with patriotic photos and framed flags, bordered on too much. He didn't think he needed to wear his commitment to country with such obvious fervor, but Selene disagreed.

It was part of her campaign to remind him just how much of her family's Old South money she'd invested in Kingston and how significant her personal stake really was. From the boys in their private high school to the family's sprawling three-story Georgian-style home in nearby Great Falls, she played the role.

He despised the personal part. Let him stay at the office, away from the ridiculous chatter and incessant arguing over things like limits on the boys' television watching and picking the "right" school activities, and his satisfaction level remained high.

Except for Sean Moore.

Glenn stepped up to the opposite side of the oversized desk. "We were unable to reach Sean's sister in Annapolis as hoped. She wasn't at her shop."

Bryce glanced at his watch a second time, even though he was very aware of the hour. "This should be the one time of the day she's there."

The businessman in him balked at the idea of an owner walking away at the busiest part of the workday. Summer in Annapolis meant tourists and profits. She ran a small business. She'd have to be insane to leave her shop during peak hours.

Glenn nodded. "I agree."

Bryce turned his pen end over end, tapping it against the desktop with each pass. "Then tell me why her shop is closed."

"The police surrounded the place."

His pen hung there, stopped in midair, when he heard the exact comment he dreaded. "Someone called the police?"

"Yes."

The last thing he needed was outside interference. "Find out who and while you're at it, find her."

Glenn swallowed hard enough for his throat to bobble. "Right."

"We find her, we find her idiot brother."

"And then?"

Bryce knew the next step. He didn't have the benefit of growing up in an expensive neighborhood lined with trees and home to rounds of nannies, which in this case would have been a detriment anyway. The Baltimore docks had taught him a thing or two about life.

"I'll handle Sean Moore."

Chapter Four

Fifteen minutes later, Pax created a false trail. He doubled back and looped around, using skills he learned long before reaching adulthood, when he'd been trying to hide from Davis after curfew and downing more beer than his dimwitted teen brain could handle. With the road behind him clear except for the usual summer traffic, Pax eased his death grip on the steering wheel and let his shoulders slump back into the seat.

He eyed up Joel and Kelsey in the backseat of the SUV. They sat on opposite sides of the vehicle, with Kelsey pressed tight against the door, her head resting on the glass.

Pax, usually comfortable with silence, felt the need to say something. "I'm hoping this next part of the plan goes better."

Joel smiled but his attention never wavered from his scan outside the window. "We have a plan?"

"Not exactly what I wanted to hear," she mumbled.

Pax eased his foot off the gas and tapped the brakes so he could make the steep turn into the driveway behind the Corcoran Team property. The bounce under the wheels had his leg shifting and his back teeth grinding together.

The ride through slim streets, historical and perfect for the charming look of the tourist town, made the trip bumpy. The constant lookout for following cars kept his focus off the road just long enough for him to hit every stupid pothole between Kelsey's shop and the team headquarters.

She rested a hand against the window. "This looks like a house, not a workplace."

Pax understood the confusion. On top of the emotional roller coaster, he drove her deeper into the heart of the historic section of Annapolis and straight up to a house sitting amid tall trees. It was a federal-style standalone and a bit imposing the way it soared three stories into the air, except for a small portion, about a third, of the top floor that functioned as an open porch area—which they never used because the site would leave them too exposed.

"Don't worry," Joel said. "It's a home on the top and office on the bottom."

Pax was done talking and ready to find a bottle of painkillers. "Let's go."

He slammed the car into Park the second he pulled into one of the open garage bays at the back of the office property. He had the door open and jumped down, hoping to walk off the big band thumping in his thigh.

The small white stones that paved the space between the separate garage and the redbrick building crunched under his shoes and further threw off his balance. Much more of this and he'd be back on crutches, and he vowed to burn those as soon as he found out where Lara had hidden them.

Lara Bart Weeks, his brand-new sister-in-law and the absolute best thing ever to happen to his big brother, Davis. He was two years older and even now off enjoying the end of his honeymoon while Pax handled the coffeehouse mess.

Not that this job was supposed to blow.

Pax had been ordered to desk duty until his leg healed. The only reason the boss let Pax handle the assignment was he threatened to shoot out the surveillance screens in the office if he had to sit there and do paperwork for one more minute. That led to a low-risk operation, a stakeout of the coffee shop. Just sitting and eating doughnuts.

In some ways, it was an easy stakeout because no one expected Sean to seek out his sister. Nothing in their relationship suggested he would, not when he was deeply mired in trouble. And boy was he. But Sean had surprised them all.

They'd gotten halfway across the open space of the yard when Connor Bowen slipped out the back door of the house and stood on the small porch, just under the overhang. He wore black dress pants and a long-sleeve blue dress shirt, and managed to blend in despite being totally out of place in the relaxed summer environment.

But that's who he was. After years in the field doing work and traveling to places Pax could only guess about, Connor craved air-conditioning and a desk.

"So much for the idea of resting the leg," he said as he crossed his arms over his chest and stared Pax down. Being only seven years older didn't keep Connor from looking every inch the in-charge boss man.

Kelsey stopped biting her lower lip and came to a halt in the clearing. Her arm shot out and she grabbed Pax's. "You really are injured?"

Connor's eyebrow lifted. "You can't tell?"

Joel snorted as he passed them all by and went straight to the back door. "I need food and the bathroom, and not in that order."

"Knock yourself out." Connor shifted to the side to let Joel pass, but then he restaked his ground. Legs braced, arms folded and hovering by the door as if to say anyone who went in had to go through him first.

Pax got secrecy and understood the operation, but they were blown. There was no way to salvage this assignment as set up and feed Kelsey some line about being legitimate agents who just happened to stumble into her coffee shop in time to rescue her.

Pax doubted any sane woman would buy the story, and he knew Kelsey was far too smart to go there. Combine that with her survival instinct, which appeared to tick in the expert range, and their options for handling this in a quick and easy manner decreased significantly.

She put her hand above her eyes and squinted against the sun as she looked Connor over. "Who are you…or am I not allowed to know that, either?"

"I take it from that response things didn't go well this morning."

Pax hid his smile. Connor knew exactly how the mess unfolded at Decadent Brew. He was tied in to the communications link, ran the unexpected removal of Kelsey from back in his office while watching his bank of monitors, and by now had placed the right calls and talked to the right people to keep the Corcoran Team's name out of this and ensure the gas leak story led the news.

That was the job. He was the handler. The guy who made it all possible behind the scenes.

"Connor Bowen, my boss." Pax put a hand low on her back, thinking to steer her inside. There was no need to stand out in the open and invite gawking.

She didn't move. "And what exactly is your job again? All of you, any of you, any response would be welcome."

Connor opened the back door. He threw out an arm and motioned toward the house. "We'll explain inside."

She hummed. The tune was quiet, almost as if it kicked on as her brain began to spin, but Pax could hear it. As a fellow under-the-breath singer, he recognized the almost imperceptible sound. And he'd heard it from her before when she made intricate coffee drinks for other customers while he waited in line for his.

He didn't know what her humming meant or why she did it, but the idea of having some extra time with her to figure it out…well, he didn't hate the idea.

Before he could push or try another attempt at issuing an order he knew she'd ignore, neither of which he wanted to do with her in this tenuous state and Connor standing right there watching, she moved. She hesitated before stepping inside, stopping to stare at the out-of-place dark square on the wall next to the back door.

A retinal scan and a handprint reader. Admittedly not the usual office setup, but he doubted she knew what she was looking at and since Connor had clearly disabled it remotely when he stepped outside, Pax didn't have to give a demonstration now.

She pointed at the pad. "More secrets, I guess?"

The woman didn't miss much. "You'll get used to it."

"Not so far."

KELSEY TRIED TO take it all in. She'd expected a fancy high-tech room filled with gadgets. She got an open kitchen, complete with blue cabinets and a huge farm sink. No food on the counters, unless you counted the two half-empty chip bags.

The really strange thing was the overabundance of coffeemakers. Not fancy ones. Normal coffeemakers…all four of them. The sight made her wonder how many people worked here, if any were women and if they ever ate regular meals. It also made the shop owner part of her think they should pay for her to provide better beverages.

A swinging door led to a wide-open space. A double room, probably what should be a combination living and dining room, but in this case housed desks and computers in individual work spaces. Closed cabinets with locks lined the far wall, and a conference room table sat in the middle of everything.

Everywhere she looked she saw television monitors, some big and some small. One looked as if it piggybacked traffic cams, with images flickering from intersection to intersection. Another showed a front door, she guessed to this address.

On the one across the room…wait.

She headed for Joel. He sat slumped in a chair, running his hand through his dark hair, with his feet on the countertop and a mug of something she guessed was coffee in his hand. Peeking over his shoulder, she watched people scurry around out front of Decadent Brew, the place where she worked and lived and worried about losing almost every day.

A couple tested the doors and then stared at the sign with the posted hours. Being closed, knowing what the loss of income and product could cost her later, had a lump clogging Kelsey's throat. Heaviness tugged at her muscles, and she had to fight the urge to sit down.

Everything she owned, all she was, centered on that building. The dark, strangely spooky building. The lights were off and something—she leaned in closer and studied the scene, maybe drapes of some sort—covered the windows.

She spun around and met Pax's emotionless gaze. "Is this your doing?"

"Mine, actually." Connor walked in, carrying a pot of coffee. He set it in the middle of the table on a tray surrounded by unused mugs.

It was all so normal yet so wrong.

"Where is everybody?" Pax dropped into a chair and blew out a long breath. He stretched his right leg out in front of him as he massaged his thigh.

She wasn't sure what caused the injury, but she believed it existed. She was about to ask him about it when she sensed a gaze on her. A quick glance at Connor and she caught the small shake of his head.

"Davis is enjoying his final days in Hawaii, as you know. The rest of the group is cleaning up the mess in Catalina, except for Ben," Connor said as he poured her a cup of coffee. "Ben is on his way to the hospital to check on your injured attacker. I'll head out in a second. Sounds like I have a very angry investigator to calm down and a few explanations I need to give."

Pax slumped down farther in the black leather chair. "I don't ever want your job."

Without turning around, Joel saluted with his cup. "Yeah, no envy over here, either."

The information collected and piled, and Kelsey tried to mentally flip through and analyze it all. The really tall, dark and businesslike one was in charge. If this Connor guy wasn't the overall boss, he should be because he acted like it and his six-foot-three-or-four height suggested no one mess with him.

The younger, black-haired, scruffy-chinned one, Joel, seemed to be connected to the monitor. There was a brother named Davis roaming around out there somewhere, some guy named Ben and a group of people, she had no idea how many, in California.

It was a lot to take in.

She grabbed on to the back of Pax's chair while a wave of dizziness crashed over her. With everything that happened during the past hour or so and the rapid-fire confusion bombarding her brain, she was fading. Fatigue crept into her muscles, and the coffee in four pots might not be enough to keep her on her feet and functioning.

As if he read her mind, Connor poured another cup, skipped the sugar and extras, and downed it black. "I'll get this worked out and then we can figure out our next steps."

The words snapped her out of the haze that had started washing through her. The conversation replayed and she wondered if they even knew they talked in code. "And the *this* in that sentence would be what?"

She was treated to three blank stares and a sudden abundance of quiet. Even Pax did a twisty-turny thing to look up and give her eye contact, but no one said a thing. A wall clock ticked somewhere and garbled noises came from the earphones Joel now had around his neck.

If she'd known such a simple question would get their joint attention, she'd have asked one an hour ago.

Connor was the first to move. He sat across from Pax and on the other side of the table from her. "The scene at your store."

"Is everyone okay?" Pax asked.

"All the good guys are."

The men were off and running again on a topic other than the one she'd introduced. They offered a snippet of information, failed to explain anything and then moved on. She never knew how annoying that was until now.

She raised a finger, but that did nothing for the balls of anxiety bouncing around inside her stomach. "Um, excuse me?"

Connor smiled. He flashed his soft blues eyes and shot her the I'm-listening stare Pax tended to use on her. Clearly whatever group all these guys worked for taught the same facial expressions in a Pacify-the-Ladies class.

"Your customers and employees are fine," Connor said. "They think there was a gas leak as cover for a burglary at another store, and you got caught up in it but are fine."

Even though she heard that sort of thing on the news every night, it sounded ridiculous when applied to her life. Anyone who knew her would expect her store to stay open, or at least for her to be out on the street giving away the unused inventory. Not that all that many people knew her, not with her work hours.

But she didn't purposely hide in her house. Not anymore. "Who told people that story?" she asked.

"Me."

She had a feeling Connor would be the one to pipe up with an answer. "Because that's your job?"

Pax laid a hand on her closed fist and brought her around to the side of his chair. "Have you seen Sean in the past few weeks?"

She ripped her fingers out of Pax's hand. As they all continued the male staring ring, her knees went soft and the ground beneath her moved in a rolling wave. Her brain tried to shut out any reference to her brother. At twenty-three he was three years younger and had spent more time than she could count in trouble.

She swallowed and cleared her throat, but the words would not come. It took a good minute before she could force out a question. "You mentioned him before. What exactly do you know about Sean?"

Pax didn't flinch. Didn't bother to look guilty or worried. He just sat there rubbing his leg. "Everything."

"How?"

He made a noise, something dismissive and all male. "Not important."

She slapped a palm on the conference table and watched his gaze move to it before bouncing back to her face.

She wasn't trying to make noise. All she wanted was to hold her body upright. "It is to me."

"Kelsey?"

Connor said her name, but she refused to look at him. She wanted Pax to tell her, to come clean and finally let her know what was happening and who he really was. "No."

A thundering silence returned to the room. This time even the clock stayed silent.

That was fine with her. Balanced on the table, she could

stand there all day. She *would* if that's what it took to make her point.

After another moment of ticking tension, Pax exhaled in that women-are-so-tiresome way men did when pushed to talk about something they wanted to ignore. "That's a shame. Finding him sooner rather than later would be safer for you."

Yeah, he still didn't get it. "I mean, no, we're not going to play it this way."

"Excuse me?" Pax's eyebrow ticked up and the last signs of the charming guy with the love of black coffee disappeared.

"You know about me, and apparently my brother, and I don't even want to know what else. Until I understand what's happening and where you all fit in, I'm not saying another thing."

"There's a limit on what we can divulge," Joel said from the relative safety of the other side of the room.

As if she was going to accept that nonsense excuse. "Then take me to the police. I'm sure they'll want to question me about this supposed theft you made up."

Pax's cheeks rushed with color and his fingers dug deeper into the arms of his chair. "No, they don't."

"I have no idea what that means."

The finger lock on his chair didn't ease. "We were hired to watch over you."

"By whom?"

Connor was already shaking his head. "We can't tell you that, but we can say we're the good guys and we're here to keep you safe."

"Because you would tell me if you were the bad guys?"

Joel chuckled. "We should check her injuries and Pax's, maybe get her a change of clothes and some food."

"I don't need—"

"Good idea." Pax struggled to his feet.

When his body started to fall again, she put an arm around

his waist and held him up. A backache settled in a second later as she wrenched her muscles and locked her knees and arms to support him. He braced his hands against the table and leaned on her.

She looked up, thinking to ask Connor for help, and saw the strain across his face. More than that, worry. These men might work together, but their bond went deeper. She wanted to curse them all for making this situation so hard on her. They expected her blind faith and gave nothing in return.

She thought about it another second and decided that wasn't true. They gave her protection, but she still wasn't clear on why she needed it.

If Pax had just stood up without trouble or had the courtesy to stay seated, she would have kept fighting him. Thanks to the mention of her injuries, every muscle and cell inside her started to ache. Talk about the power of suggestion.

But the real problem was Pax.

Her gaze traveled over him. Over the way he kept weight off his right leg and the cut along his cheek. If the clenched jaw were any indication, he was in pain. She was confused and angry, but the guy who stormed in to save her, protected her from a crushing fall and killed for her looked unsteady on his feet and ready to drop.

It was the wake-up call she didn't want but couldn't ignore. She swallowed back the rest of her questions and fell deep into appreciation mode. She didn't know him but she owed him.

She faced Connor and skipped over the stuff she wanted to know to the stray comment that caught her attention. "You have women's clothes here?"

His white-knuckle grip on the edge of the table tightened. "My wife's."

Now, there was a bit of news she didn't see coming that

sent her gaze zipping to the thin band on Connor's finger. "Where is she?"

"Out of town."

Yet another person not there. That appeared to be the norm around this house…or office…or whatever it was. "Fine. If someone checks Pax's injuries, I'll clean up, then you can all decide that I deserve to know more and start talking."

Pax snorted. "Wrong."

Before that minute she'd forgotten she held on to him. She gave his waist a reassuring squeeze and then dropped her arm. "That's the only solution I'll accept."

Joel glanced at Connor. "Told you."

He nodded. "You're right."

They'd lost her in all the partial sentences. "What are you two talking about?"

Joel shot her a huge smile as he stood up. "Don't you worry. I'll take care of Pax."

"You're qualified?"

If possible that smile grew even wider. "Yes, ma'am."

"Well, I don't agree to the schedule." Pax practically snarled when he said the words.

Tough.

This time Connor stood. Something about the way he moved had all eyes focused on him. "I do. The lady is—"

"Kelsey," she said.

Connor gave her a nod. "Kelsey is right. Pax gets treatment, she gets changed and a once-over for injuries, and we meet back here in thirty. No arguments."

Pax pushed off the table and stood up straight. His large frame wobbled but he didn't fall this time. He didn't match his friends' smiles with one of his own, either.

When he looked at her, his mouth had fallen into a flat line. "One thing you should know."

Dread tumbled through her. "What?"

"We control all the doors and windows, so there's no way for you to escape once you're up there."

Honestly, the man was clueless. She'd turned that corner when a third attacker showed up and a bullet whizzed by her head. "Why would you think I would try?"

"Experience."

Chapter Five

Dan Breckman appeared in Bryce's office doorway shortly after three that afternoon. He carried a file and wore a scowl. Neither of those proved unusual for the man. He was sixty, retired military and a constant nuisance.

"We have a problem."

Bryce tried to mentally count the times Dan had wandered out of his corner office and said that each week. Whatever the number, Bryce didn't have time for his nonsense now. "I have a phone conference in a few minutes."

"This can't be ignored."

Bryce tapped his pen against his keyboard and cursed his decision to hire Dan as a consultant. With his knowledge and reputation, the man added a level of legitimacy to the new intelligence division as it fought its way through a corporate field loaded with big players, but he was far too used to being in charge. He turned out to be the hands-on type rather than that sit-quietly-and-collect-a-check type, as Bryce had hoped.

Dan failed the keep-your-enemies-closer test. Giving him the office turned out to be a fatal mistake. Access to programs and business plans was one thing, but Dan tried to worm his way into every aspect of the new operations, including personnel issues, which were out of his purview. Bryce said no, but people in the workplace talked. Shared information.

And when Dan started asking questions about the one subject for which Bryce did not have a satisfactory answer, telling the older man to get back to work only solved part of the problem. Bryce could push Dan off but that didn't solve the Sean issue.

Dan didn't wait for a conversation opening. He stepped up and hovered on the other side of Bryce's desk. "Sean Moore didn't show up for work again today. That's sixteen weekdays in a row."

Bryce knew exactly how long it had been. Right down to the minute, and he could feel each one tick by inside him. Hear the knocking in his head.

The click of the pen beat into one long, rapid-fire drumming line. "I had human resources use all of our contact information to find him. It would appear he left town."

"In light of his history, I can't say this is a surprise, but I continue to be confused about how he was hired and why he was put on my team."

Each accusatory word scraped against the inside of Bryce's brain, inflaming the anger already burning there. He shouldn't have to handle hiring at the lower levels, to oversee every bothersome detail. He had too much work to do running the company without sitting in on the interviews of every petty administrative assistant and mailroom clerk.

From now on Glenn would have that task. With his charts and spreadsheets, he would be in charge of ensuring that stupid mistakes like this never happened again. Either that or he'd lose his job.

But Bryce had no intention of sharing any responsibility with Dan. "You're referencing Sean's father's history. Sean's academic record and criminal history were perfect."

"He failed his recent lie detector test."

A fact Bryce had buried but Dan had clearly uncovered. While he was investigating this matter, ripping it apart and dissecting every piece of paper, every line, Bryce would look into Dan's role, as well. The man knew too much, too quickly, and Bryce vowed to find out where the information leak in his office came from.

"I am aware of young Sean's test. As the owner of this company—" Bryce emphasized the word *owner,* letting the syllables bounce off his tongue "—I am advised immediately of this sort of thing. When an employee's clearance is revoked, since the clearance is a condition of employment, the job position is pulled, as well."

"But this young man conducted preliminary computer work on the new Signal Reconnaissance Program *before* his security clearance had been approved."

Another piece of information Dan should not know. Each word moved him closer to the top of Bryce's things-to-handle list. "And if the time comes, I will contact NCIS."

Bryce had spent his youth being pushed around, but those days were long behind him. He dropped his pen on the desk, letting it thud against the wood, before he stood. He stretched every vertebra as he straightened to full height. Dan may have worn a uniform, but Bryce had the sort of shield that came with harsh and unwanted life experience.

"You're depending on my reputation to open doors for the company at the Pentagon." Dan dropped the file on the desk and balanced his fists on each side of it, allowing him to lean in close across the expanse. "That gives me some rights, including the right to question employment choices."

Dan's point about needing an "in" at the Pentagon wasn't wrong. Starting tomorrow, Bryce would begin the search for another consultant to handle that. One satisfied to collect a check and confine his work to wining and dining former colleagues. Someone who would know when to shut up.

"You know, Dan, I get that you're used to a certain chain of command and being at the top of it, but that's not where you are now. I do not answer to you nor do I appreciate your interference."

A tense silence followed the comment. It took a few seconds for Dan to relax the grim line of his mouth. "Fine."

He pushed the file across the desk.

Bryce didn't make a move toward it. In this game, he would not be the one to blink. "What exactly is that?"

"All the intel I gathered on Sean Moore and his family." A small smile played on his mouth. Gone was the blank stare and muscle twitch in his cheek. "You're not the only one with connections."

"Which is supposed to mean what?"

"Just trying to make sure we have an understanding. An investigation into Kingston and the issue about having a non-cleared individual working prematurely on a top-secret project, even in the planning stages, could be a problem for the company's contracting status with the government. That's why I am willing, you could even say insisting, that I be allowed to help resolve this."

The threat wasn't an empty one. There were laws associated with entering into contracts with the government and lists of rules to follow. Bryce didn't flinch. Didn't even blink. "I'll consider the request."

Minutes turned into hours before Pax made it downstairs again. He took the last few steps from the second floor without letting up on his death grip on the stair railing. His sneakered feet fell with heavy thuds, but at least he could still walk. While standing under the scalding shower spray twenty minutes ago, he doubted he'd be able to maneuver his body to get where he needed to be. Relief replaced his growing headache when he realized he'd been wrong.

He limped into the main workroom, ignoring the plates piled on the table's edge. They'd switched the afternoon agenda and eaten first. With limited conversation except for Joel's ongoing commentary about the movies he'd recently seen, the food went down easy, and Pax no longer worried Kelsey would dive out the window at the first chance. Yeah, she'd promised previously, but watching her smile and laugh and never once scan the room for an exit convinced him.

After the shower and rounds of unnecessary medical attention, Pax now had a rebandaged thigh from his old gunshot wound and a constant dull ache that flared into full-blown raging pain when he put too much weight on that side. Made walking tough but not impossible. The treatment combined with clean clothes, and he felt ready to go again.

But he planned to do it from a seated position for the next hour or so. He dropped into the closest chair and leaned back into the soft leather. A quick glance around the room started a buzzing in his head. "Where's Kelsey?"

"Calm down." Joel walked in from the kitchen and exchanged a new pot of coffee for the old one. "She's upstairs."

"Good…and I'm fine. Perfectly calm." Except for the adrenaline kick that still had his heart triple-timing. Pax closed his eyes and tried to steady the beat.

"Uh-huh."

At the hint of amusement in Joel's voice, Pax's eyes popped open again. He shot his friend a you're-on-the-edge frown. "Don't do that."

"The woman has you spinning."

Spinning. Fantasizing. Forgetting his training. Losing control. All of that. "She tried to run before, so I was just checking."

"Which brings up another point." Joel balanced a thigh on the conference room table. Sat right there, a few feet away from Pax, and talked with a thread of laughter in his voice. "Your lady skills need help. You now have them all but jumping out of cars to get away from you."

"I was watching over her."

"Oh, I noticed."

"There's nothing else between us but the job. That's it." Pax repeated the lines over and over in his head, as he'd been doing for days, and he still didn't buy them. He'd moved beyond watching for danger and started just plain watching her a week ago.

Joel closed one eye and looked at the ceiling as if pretending to count. "So many words in that denial."

"I can think of two words for you."

Joel laughed out loud that time. "Man, don't make me say 'uh-huh' again."

Letting out a long, exaggerated exhale, Pax gave in. "Clearly, you have something to say. Get to it."

"I see the way you look at her." Some of the amusement left Joel's voice this time. He spoke lower, quieter.

Pax knew he all but drooled in Kelsey's presence and hated that Joel had noticed the weakness. "I'm watching to see if she's going to bolt and whether I'm going to get injured running after her."

"Nope, that's not it."

Since hitting the subject head-on didn't appear to be working, Pax went for the obvious parry. "Where's Connor?"

Joel tapped his thumb against the rim of his mug. "Are we changing the subject?"

"Definitely."

Joel got up from the conference table and headed for his usual desk, the one lined with monitors and other assorted equipment. "Connor headed out to play cleanup, then was meeting up with Ben to see if they could identify your attackers. The one you stabbed and put in the hospital is still out but he has to wake up sometime."

"Let's hope."

"Ben is standing guard, just in case." A rhythmic clicking

filled the room as Joel tapped on the keyboard and sent the one monitor flipping through streets around the historic district. "Any chance Kelsey is involved in her brother's mess?"

Joel dropped the question without fanfare. Just put it out there and dragged that elephant right to the middle of the room.

Still… "Excuse me?"

Joel shrugged. "You said yourself you don't know her. You've just been watching her. She could be Sean's partner."

"That's not true." Pax refused to let the doubt take hold in his mind.

"My mistake. I guess you know this woman better than I thought."

But he didn't, and that was one of the problems.

Chapter Six

"Sounds like I'm interrupting something important," Kelsey said in a near whisper.

Pax almost jumped out of his chair. Forget the increased heart rate. Every cell inside him whipped into a frenzy at the surprise sound of her voice until he had to grab on to the chair to stay in it.

She'd snuck up on them. *Them*. The undercover operatives with all the training. No way that happened without her trying to make it happen, which made him wonder what information she'd hoped to overhear.

Then there was her outfit. Frayed gym shorts and a trim white tee. She smelled sweet, like fruit. He had no idea what women used in the shower to make their skin glow, but Kelsey had found some of it. Even now the ends of her long hair curled as they dried.

A man could take only so much before he had to dunk his head in a bucket of ice water, and Pax was right on the edge. "It was nothing."

She shot him that look women gave when they knew they had the upper hand. "Oh, it was something. Care to tell me what?"

"Kelsey." Joel stood up. Even cleared his throat, but that didn't hide the sudden flush to his skin. "How are you feeling?"

"Nice try at throwing me off, what with that make-the-ladies-swoon smile and all, but answer the question." She could have picked any chair. She headed straight for the one next to Pax. "One of you, both of you, I don't care."

The compliment about Joel went overboard, in Pax's view. He was about to point that out when she started walking and talking, and something about that combination left him speechless, if only for a second.

Joel started to put his earphones on. "Once Connor gets back—"

She sighed at them. "No."

Joel froze. "What?"

Pax weighed the risks. There was protocol for this type of situation, but they'd already blown through the rules by bringing her here. The hide-and-seek portion of the day was over. If she had information, he needed it and wanted her to give it up without the games. "Sean disappeared with top-secret information."

The front two legs of Joel's chair hit the hardwood floor with a crack. "Pax, what the—"

"She deserves to know, and she's not going to take 'it's nothing' or some big stall for an answer." Pax had already tried that game and failed. Kelsey was not a woman to push to the side and feed trite lines so she'd stay quiet.

"Thanks for recognizing I'm not an idiot," she mumbled under her breath.

Pax didn't bother whispering. "It would be easier if you were."

"That's charming."

Since that wasn't his goal at the moment, the comment didn't bother him at all. "Do you know about Sean's job at Kingston Inc.?"

"We are not exactly on speaking terms, but you probably know that, too."

There was no use in denying it. Pax had read the files. They all had. "I have some information about your past."

"Like how my dad wrote bogus insurance policies for people then took their money and left them with no coverage? It's a lovely family story, one Sean thinks is a mistake. He refuses to listen to reason or look at the evidence, and there's a ton of that."

"Those details were in the news." Joel kept hitting that computer key. "The fraud case was pretty famous."

"Well, living through it was not exactly a joy. Sean remembers pieces only. I had just turned seventeen. He was thirteen and his mother fed him a constant line about how the Moore family was being oppressed by jealous poor people. I was the evil stepchild from the forgettable first marriage, so I was shut out of her little us-against-the-world club."

Pax knew all these pieces, right down to how her father spent less than two years in prison thanks to later "found" evidence implicating his assistant. They traded places and her father returned to his wife and her family money, leaving Kelsey alone.

The cycle sounded familiar. The numbness and pain. His own mother had dealt him those dual blows. Different circumstances, but abandonment was abandonment regardless of the specifics. "I understand."

"No offense but I doubt it." Her eyebrow lifted and her voice dripped with disbelief.

"I know about bad parents." Knew, lived through and somehow survived them, which was all a credit to Davis. As they were passed from relative to relative, from trailer parks to shacks unfit for humans, Davis held them together.

The idea of Kelsey not having someone like Davis to protect her made Pax's stomach lurch.

"Now I'm dying to ask about your life." The hard edge left her voice and her eyes.

Understandable, but there was no way Pax was going down that emotional road. His past left him closed-off and he preferred it that way. "Finish your story."

She gnawed on her bottom lip a second before continuing. "Sean wanted to believe our father, but I knew better. He had to touch every check that came into the office. There's no way his office manager set him up. My father lied. He went to jail then got lucky. Now he's out and that's all the time I want to spend talking about him."

Fair enough. She'd shared and now so would he.

Ignoring the shake of Joel's head, Pax explained. "Sean got a low-level job at Kingston, a communications firm that's moved into government contracting. He did some computer work and now he's missing."

There it was. Out in the open. Over Joel's eye rolling and the vivid memory of Connor's training and specific warnings about confidentiality, Pax had spilled more than he should. She had to be satisfied now.

Her head tipped to the side and her damp hair fell over her shoulder. "What piece are you leaving out?"

Apparently not. "What?"

"Why do you think he is?" Joel asked.

"Because he's assuming Sean did something wrong rather than assuming he's hurt or on vacation or something.... Or is my family name the reason you're jumping to conclusions?" Her focus never left Pax. Her gaze searched his face, and her attention did not waver. "I'm wondering if you're looking at my father's crimes and condemning Sean and maybe me."

"I never said that." That wasn't who Pax was. Not how he operated.

She traced an invisible pattern over the tabletop with her finger. "You wouldn't be the first person to make that logic leap."

"Stop painting me as the bad guy here." Pax put his hand

over hers and didn't let go when she tried to pull away. "I don't think you're involved. I also don't think your brother is hurt. Not yet, but his actions, innocent or not, put him in grave danger."

"The computer logs, the same ones Sean tried to destroy and would have succeeded if he'd known about the automatic backup he'd triggered, show he downloaded proprietary corporate material before he walked out the office door," Joel said. "Problem is the military views the stolen material as theirs, which means Sean's actions have national security implications."

She started shaking her head before Joel finished his sentence. "No way. He's immature and has made mistakes—believe me when I say I get that—but Sean would never betray his country."

"I'm not accusing him of that, but I am saying the surveillance tapes show he did everything without anyone standing over him with a gun, so we need to assume he had a reason to take what he took and figure out what it was," Joel said.

Her hollow cheeks and vacant eyes mirrored her shock. "I can't imagine Sean doing this on his own or at all."

"He emptied his bank account and canceled utilities then climbed in a car and raced out of the office parking lot." Pax couldn't let her hope of a simple misunderstanding grow, so he rushed the words out. "Does that sound like a guy who got kidnapped?"

She blinked so fast she looked as if she'd been hit in the head. "You seem to have a lot of details. Exactly who are you guys?"

This time when she tried to move her hand, Pax let her go. "We conduct high-priority but under-the-radar kidnap-rescue missions. Our clients are the government and private industry."

"You're kidding."

"We try to set up training and maneuvers to ensure kidnappings don't occur in the first place, but people don't always listen to us, which leads to the rescues. You'd be amazed how many times a corporation will send an employee into a dangerous situation without any prep."

Joel made a sound between a scoff and a huff. "Pax, really. You've said more than enough."

Pax held up his hand. He kept his gaze locked on hers and blocked Joel and his protests right out. "This time the government hired us. See, someone reported Sean's behavior and missing data to the Department of Defense. No one at Kingston has filed an official report yet, but we know."

She jerked in her chair. "What are you saying?"

Pax had come this far and refused to pretty it up now. This was a serious game, a deadly one, and the men would keep coming until and unless the Corcoran Team ferreted this out. "We don't know who the bad guys are or how far they'll go to find Sean, which is why I was watching you at Decadent Brew."

"And probably why those men attacked you. You're a link to Sean, which suggests he's still on the run and, for now, safe. We plan to keep you and him that way." The flat tone of resignation in Joel's voice was tough to miss.

"And my father?"

"Our orders are to watch you and protect Sean. That's it." Pax guessed the FBI already had someone watching over the father thanks to his criminal past.

She looked between the men with her mouth opening and closing. It took a few times before any sound escaped. "You have to admit this is a pretty unbelievable story."

"Is it? Look around you." Pax had heard so much worse. Only a few months ago he watched his boat explode at the marina as someone tried to kill Davis and Lara. Terrible things happened all the time, even in a place as idyllic as

Annapolis. "I mean, with what you've lived through with your dad and how he weaseled out of the conviction, and with what you see in this room, is it really that impossible to imagine there's a group that does what we do?"

She pushed her chair back, putting a good foot between her stomach and the table. "Why didn't you tell me all this before?"

Joel gave the keyboard one last loud tap. "We're not supposed to be telling you now."

"What does that mean?"

That was a problem for another time. Pax's instincts screamed at him to take this step. He was willing to take the hit from Connor if it came to that. Pax loved this job, in part because the government red tape and paperwork he hated so much at the DIA didn't bind him here. But this was one of those times he needed loose strings.

"We weren't sure how much you knew about your brother's activities," Pax explained.

"Meaning, you thought I might be involved in whatever he did, whatever happened, at this company."

There was that smart-woman thing again. Pax sensed that would trip him up a lot when dealing with Kelsey. She would not be easy to fool. He was starting to wonder if she'd be hard to leave.

He pushed that thought out of his head. "At the time, possibly."

"And now?"

"I just told you everything about us and the case, didn't I? That should tell you everything you need to know about my trust in you."

The lip-chewing thing started again. Much more of that and she'd start bleeding. He was just about to point that out when she jumped in. "We need to go back to the shop. To my house."

Pax sighed inside, careful not to let the noise out. He got it. It had kicked at his gut to lose the boat. It exploded with all his possessions, but he'd never cared about stuff. The loss went deeper than that. The boat was a part of him. He'd scrubbed it, cleaned it, refurbished it. Being on the open water gave him a needed sense of freedom, a break from the difficult situations he dealt with every single day, and losing it was like having that freedom snatched away.

For Kelsey the loss could be even bigger. He'd lost one thing. He couldn't imagine walking away from his home and his work at the same time. She had to be stewing in her chair over the loss of control, but, for now, that had to happen. "Kelsey, listen. I know how important work is to you. I've seen you there. But it's not safe for you right now."

"I get that." Her eyes looked clear, and she was calm.

He had no idea where she was going with this. "Then you know you can't stay there. Let's hunker down here and relax."

"You don't understand. I'm not talking about staying there. We need to retrieve the package Sean sent me."

Joel jumped out of his chair and came over to stand next to Kelsey. "What?"

Pax understood the shock. It was rumbling through him from head to foot right now. "Not possible."

"Yeah, it actually is. But now I'm wondering why you would say it that way." She crossed her arms in front of her. Even made a "hmm?" sound.

Pax's response was automatic. "No reason."

She homed in on him, angling her chair to face Pax and give Joel more of a side-to-back view. "Pax?"

He could see Joel over her shoulder. His gestures mimicked his response. "Don't do it, man."

Pax shut down the internal mental battle and blocked Joel's suggestion. He'd gone this far and stopping now didn't make much sense. "We've monitored your mail from the beginning, within days of Sean not showing up for work."

Her cheeks puffed in and out. "You...did..."

"Yeah."

"That's just spectacular." She tipped her head back and stared at the ceiling.

"The word you want is *necessary.*"

Joel swore under his breath as he shot Pax an open-mouthed, bewildered look. "When did you get so chatty?"

Pax refused to back down. "Do you really think we would have gotten anything done unless we told her the truth?"

"Thanks for that. I think." She dropped her head again, looking back and forth between them, as if analyzing to see the best way to get the answer she wanted. "Now that you shared, I will. The package came with an inventory delivery but didn't have a carrier tag on it. I thought it was weird at the time but figured something had gotten mixed up somewhere."

Pax tried to figure out where they had a hole in security and couldn't picture it. He'd hand that one over to Connor to ferret out. "What was in the box?"

"That's just it. I didn't open it."

"You weren't curious?" Joel asked.

"Sean and I aren't close. I made the choice long ago not to race around after him."

"I still don't get it."

Pax appreciated Joel saying what they were both feeling.

"He'd sent stuff before. Stuff to make me feel guilty, about our father and his health. Stuff from our childhood."

Pax was starting to hate her family. Thinking about her in that house, with her mother dead from cancer and her father immediately remarried to a younger woman with obvious social-climbing expectations, made everything inside Pax squeeze and tense. He wanted to hit something. "Sounds like a great guy."

"Yeah, well. He *is* in trouble now, isn't he?"

That was enough family talk. Pax needed her mind back on the box. "You think the delivery could mean something."

"Now that I put the timing together. It came a few days before you started showing up at the shop."

Joel threw his hands in the air. "There's your answer."

She ignored him and pointed at Pax. "And before you start issuing orders and throwing your weight around on that bad leg, I'm coming with you to retrieve it."

She'd clearly lost her mind.

"No."

"You dragged me out of the shop. Now you're stuck with me." She glanced at his leg. "Besides, I think I can run faster than you at the moment."

Pax didn't realize he'd been rubbing the injury until he followed her gaze and looked at his thigh. Great, he now massaged it without thinking. "Those are fighting words."

"You take me or I scream loud enough to bring the police running."

A trickle of unease sliced through him. "I thought you didn't want to escape."

"I don't, but you're not escaping me, either."

He could live with that.

SEAN RAN THROUGH the series of dark parking lots scattered under the Whitehurst Freeway. The Potomac River sat off to his left and the noise and traffic of Georgetown ran a few blocks up to his right. He'd been on the move long enough he didn't care about either.

As the humidity slammed into him and sweat soaked through his jeans and drenched his tee under his backpack, his entire focus centered on how he'd messed up. Ending up in the one part of Washington, D.C., without Metro access proved to be a huge tactical mistake. So much for the theory of using the computer lab at George Washington University and getting in and out and finding the information he needed on who was screwing him over back at Kingston. That's where he'd started but he was nowhere near there now.

He'd bypassed the security by swiping some student's access card and then lain low until the classrooms shut down one by one. He'd even used the password workaround he set up in the Kingston system for emergencies, the one that couldn't be traced back to him, but the echoing footsteps in the hall and the two guys walking around who looked more like they could lift a garbage truck than that they were part of the late-night cleaning staff ruined everything.

He'd been ducking, hiding and running ever since. And now it was getting dark, which would help hide his presence but make progress even tougher.

Instead of heading toward Dupont Circle as he should have done coming out of GW, he'd made his way to Georgetown and now he was stuck. Kelsey wasn't answering her phone, and he didn't have the cash for a bus ticket or a car to get to Annapolis.

No way could he use anything in his name. Credit cards and ATMs were out and the money he withdrew at the beginning of this mess weeks ago was running out. Getting more wouldn't work because the transaction would be tracked in a second.

They were everywhere, watching and following.

But there was one other place he could go. One person he could trust. Not the guy who dragged him into this mess with big promises. Someone else. It would take the last of his cash to get there, but he didn't have a choice.

Chapter Seven

Kelsey doubted her decision to tag along with Pax almost from the second she suggested it. More like, insisted on it. So much for his comments about her being so smart. Now, two hours later, she stumbled around at dusk as she stalked her own building.

Yeah, this was a normal evening.

They walked down the street, starting several town houses away from her storefront and scanning the area as they went. She grabbed a fistful of Pax's shirt from behind and wedged her body under his arm, hoping the move looked loving to anyone who might be watching, but really she just wanted him close. He'd proved to be the right guy to have around when the bullets started flying, though she hoped they were done with that…forever.

When he zigzagged to shift out of the shine of the overhead flickering streetlamps, he took her with him. They were far enough from the City Dock to avoid most of the tourist and late-dinner traffic, but people still passed by, some stopping to gawk in the windows of the businesses a block away.

Then there was his limp. Add that to the panic churning in her stomach, and she couldn't help but second-guess every decision she'd made today. And had it really been that morning when the thugs attacked her and Pax rushed in?

No matter the number of hours, her nerve endings wouldn't

stop jumping. She kept glancing behind them just in case. It was as if her skin suddenly shrank to a size too small, and all she wanted to do was pull and tug and get someplace where she could sit down, close her eyes and not fear being shot.

She hated the twitchy, panicked feeling rolling over her. But she had no one else to blame. By mentioning the box to Joel and Pax, she'd all but guaranteed a trip back to her house. It sounded like a great idea when it first rolled off her tongue. Now, in the growing dark with hidden corners everywhere, not so much.

Ignoring the sticky heat, she cuddled in closer to Pax's side, stretching up to whisper in his ear. "Retrieving this box was a fundamentally terrible idea. I'm sorry I even mentioned it."

"You said that already." He slipped an arm around her and rested his palm on the small of her back. "Three times, actually."

"Maybe the fourth will convince you."

He treated her to one of those warm smiles that had his eyes twinkling. Man, she loved that look. It managed to be sweet and hot at the same time, and it wiped away a good portion of her growing dread along with her common sense.

Her cheeks warmed as his gaze roamed over her face. "What is it?" she asked.

"Joel and I can do this without you." Pax stared at her lips as he said the words. "You can wait in the car or go back at the house. Connor should be there soon."

Lost in the husky sound of Pax's voice, she almost missed the comment. "Joel is already back in the office, heading up the comm."

Pax reached over and rubbed a finger along her chin. "Didn't take you long to pick up the work lingo."

"I'd like to take credit but I'm only repeating what Joel said."

As if on cue, Joel's deep voice echoed in her head. "And I'm in your ear and can hear everything, so keep it clean you two. Or not. I'm flexible and happy to listen in."

Her hand went to her ear, and she glanced around to see if anyone else could hear the voice. "That's an odd sensation."

Pax shrugged. "You get used to it."

"That's not what you normally say." Joel chuckled as he talked. "I usually hear a lot of swearing and complaining. Then you tell me I should shut the—"

Pax cleared his throat. "Correction, you get used to ignoring Joel. That's what I meant to say."

They were one town house away from her building, the same one she'd scraped clean of wallpaper and then painted and loved even as it sucked every cent out of her bank account. Pax's tempo didn't change. His shoes tapped against the sidewalk in a steady beat, a weird rhythmic clicking that eased the pounding in her temples.

When she concentrated on the sound, she picked up something else—a slight drag on every other step that matched with a tensing in his jaw.

Her hand pressed against the firm muscles of his back. "How's the leg?"

The last of his sexy smile fell. "Fine."

"The stress lines around your mouth suggest otherwise."

His fingers clenched against her. "Those come from having to answer the question every hour or so."

Before this morning she might have let the subject go, assume she was out of line and feel guilty for asking. But so much had happened within hours and so little was in her control that she grabbed on to what she could. "Is your curt response supposed to get me to drop the topic?"

"Actually, yes."

"That's not going to work."

"You're like a female version of Joel."

"For the record, I'm not sure he means that as a compliment," Joel said, his voice crisp and clear inside her head.

When they crossed the small open space between her building and the legal firm next door, her steps hesitated, but Pax's arm against her back propelled her forward. The move didn't make much sense. "I don't understand."

"Keep moving. Look forward or look at me like I'm the best-looking thing you've ever seen."

He kind of was. Not in the pretty-boy way. No, he didn't possess that scrubbed-clean, out-of-a-prep-school-manual rich-boy look. He was all man—rough around the edges, tall and lean with a swagger that overtook that limp.

He was the guy who protected all and stayed fiercely loyal to the rare few people he let into his life and loved. She barely knew him and she knew all of that was true.

They broke off the conversation until the only sound came from their shoes and a random car horn blocks away. Right as they passed the large front window of her shop, he turned his head and coughed.

They were a full building past hers before he spoke again. "Nothing obvious going on in there, though it's hard to see through the paper Connor put over the windows."

The whole scenario struck her as out of context. Her mind immediately went to one word: subterfuge. If Pax was trying to stop the conversation, it worked...temporarily. "Want to tell me how it happened? The leg, I mean."

He frowned at her. "Now? Really?"

"Yes, really." When he looked as if he was going to roll his eyes, she aimed for fat but couldn't find any, so she gave the skin on his back a little pinch.

"Fine." He winced and the word came out through clenched teeth. "I got shot."

Only Pax could boil down something so big into three little words. No way was that the whole story. "That's it?"

"It was a pretty big deal at the time."

"With a gun?"

His footsteps faltered. "How else does one get shot?"

"You're serious?"

"Very." There was no space between her building and the one on this side. He guided her past the window of the tailoring and backed her up against the bricks. His hands went to the wall on each side of her head as he leaned in.

"Well, that getting-shot thing is not comforting at all." Neither was the thing where she kept swallowing and her breath wheezed out of her as if a tight band constricted her chest.

"I generally manage not to get shot, if that helps."

This part of their act had her head spinning until she had to hold on to him for balance. Putting her hands against his chest sent a flush of warmth through her entire body. "Strangely, no."

She was about to say something when a car raced down the narrow street. A boy hung out the back window and whistled as he went past. A round of nasty catcalls followed. The engine continued to rev and the laughter floated all around them. The tires squealed as the driver took the corner too fast at the end of the block.

Even ignoring the annoying horny-boy part of what just happened, she tried to remember a time when she felt that free. She couldn't come up with an instance.

Pax put a hand under her chin and turned her face back to his. "Look, you're safe with me."

"I know that."

His head snapped back. "Then what's with the questions?"

"I was more concerned about how much pain you must be in. We probably shouldn't be out running around until you have a chance to rest."

"Oh."

"Interesting response. It probably says something about the women you hang out with."

His face fell. Every muscle shifted and his expression went blank. "Here we go."

She'd almost forgotten why they came. If that was his plan, to tie her insides up in a twisty knot and cause her brain to hiccup, then he'd succeeded. "Now?"

The warmth surrounding her dissipated as he inched his way back toward her building, with only his fingertips reaching out to still touch her. This time he hugged the wall and played only in the shadows.

"Looks clear from here," Joel said, breaking into the relative quiet.

Worse than forgetting to panic, she'd forgotten all about Joel and his front-row seat to the conversation with Pax. The heat hitting her cheeks could probably light the street.

But a stray thought found its way through the embarrassment. "Where exactly do you have cameras that you can see in my shop and house?"

"Don't worry." The click of a computer keyboard pounded over Joel's words. "Nowhere interesting."

Only a man would see that as a good answer. "Again, you guys need to work on your comfort skills."

"I'd rather work on speed." Pax's fingers laced through hers as he tugged her closer, right to the edge of the building where it turned down the narrow alley next to her building. "Let's move it."

"Hold up. Looks like you've got one moving in behind the building." A few minutes ticked by with Joel's breathing being the only noise on the open line. "He's leaning against the wall right outside her back door, the one that leads upstairs rather than the one that goes into the shop."

Pax shifted and his knee buckled but he regained his balance a beat later. "There's only one guy back there?"

"Is it Sean?" she asked. Her brother had visited that one time more than six months ago, so he knew where she lived. The position at the "right" back door suggested some level of knowledge about the layout of the building.

"Only if he aged ten years and put on about fifty pounds of muscle," Joel said.

Pax glanced over his shoulder at her. "Oh, okay. Now I see what you mean about the things we say and the lack-of-comfort thing."

"Told you." She rested her forehead in the deep groove between his shoulder blades. The sexy spot, the scent of his skin and heat rolling off his body, refueled her. Gave her strength when she didn't even know hers was running low. "Now what?"

Pax gave her one of those shrugs that suggested he thought the answer was obvious. "I take him out."

"Assume he has a partner."

Joel's warning had barely settled in her brain when Pax took off. She held on to his shirt and used it to stop his momentum. "Wait a second."

He turned around, which snapped her hold. He found her hand and covered it with his as he pressed it against her chest. "Do not move."

Before she could get out a warning or pull him in close and hold him there, he pivoted and headed down the dark alley in a crouch. His right foot seemed to skim across the ground as he moved without making a sound.

Forget the loose gravel and few cans. He dodged it all and ended with his back flattened against the bricks at the far end, closest to the back service alley.

With the darkening sky she couldn't see everything, but she thought she spied a gun in his hand. The anxiety pinging around inside her like a pinball gone wild increased until the balls bounced hard against her rib cage.

She shifted her weight, moved forward and then stepped back again. Seeing him peek around the corner and brace his body for attack brought home how real the danger was. Because of her. No, because of Sean and her family and whatever new disaster they'd tripped and fell into now.

Pax stepped in and saved her. Yes, it was his job, but that didn't mean she didn't owe him.

He lurched and spun around the corner, out of sight. She heard shouts and grunts and what sounded like shoes scuffing against the ground. It was enough to get her moving.

She took off down the alley, skimming her hands along the close-in walls and ignoring whatever she kept stepping on. Near the end, her ankle overturned and she stumbled, her shoulder smacking against the bricks and scraping her bare skin.

The sound of Joel's voice finally penetrated her mind. "Stop, Kelsey. Now."

She ignored the warning, blocked out everything except the screaming in her brain that told her to get to Pax and help however she could. She kicked something hard and heard metal clank. Dropping down, she felt around for whatever she hit, hoping she could use it as a weapon. But the sound of male pounding male had her standing up again.

She slipped around the corner as the noise grew louder. She watched as they rolled across the concrete. The attacker wore all black and had dark hair, but she could see the sweat dripping from his forehead when he wrestled Pax's back to the ground.

They punched and kicked. The attacker landed a vicious shot to Pax's stomach that had him coughing even as he swore. The attacker was on top of Pax with hands wrapped around his throat. Pax bucked his body and swiveled his head from side to side, but the other man was choking the air out of him.

Tension swirled around her as she raced over to the trash bin, looking for something—anything—to knock the attacker out. Joel kept shouting but she could make out only the word *wait,* the one thing she knew she couldn't afford to do.

She turned back around, helpless and empty-handed, determined to crash into the attacker and at least buy Pax a few seconds of air. What happened after that she had no clue. She started the mental countdown and headed for the confusing pile of arms and legs. Through the thrashing, Pax glared at her. His eyes told her to back away, but this time he was the one who needed protection.

She would not let him down.

Right when she would have kicked out or climbed on the stranger's back, Pax's strength seemed to double. He lifted his back off the ground and slammed a fist right into the attacker's face. The man dropped like dead weight on top of Pax.

The whole thing unspooled in seconds, but she couldn't take it in. Couldn't get her feet to move or her breathing to restart. He'd been at the edge of death and now acted as if he'd been toying with the guy the whole time.… Had he?

Joel's voice broke into the silence. "Someone talk to me."

Pax pushed and shoved until the other man fell to the side. Sitting up, Pax wiped a hand across his mouth and a red smear stained the back. He shook his head. "He's down but it was too easy."

"Sure seemed quick," Joel said.

What was happening? "Are you both crazy? The guy was choking Pax."

"You were supposed to stay out front." With one hand balanced against the ground, Pax pushed up to his feet. His right leg stayed bent as he rolled his shoulders back. "The deal in bringing you along was that you would do what we say."

"I thought you were in trouble." Even to her ears she thought her voice rang hollow.

His teeth clamped together as he stepped over the downed body to get to her. "So, you came running?"

"You wanted me to leave?"

His eyes twinkled but not in a flirty way. In a way that flashed fire. "I want you to stay alive."

"Kids, we still have a problem and a job to do," Joel said.

Pax fought off a bruiser who outweighed him by more than a few pounds and yet they acted as if they'd lost this battle. She would never understand men. "I hate to ask what that means."

"We likely have a partner around here somewhere. Hard to imagine there's only one guy out here ready to cause trouble. Guys like this usually work in pairs." Pax bent over and searched the attacker's pockets and came away with a phone but nothing else. Pax whipped a white plastic tie out of his pocket.

"What are you doing?" Her real question had to do with how most people didn't carry those things around with them.

"Keeping him quiet for a few minutes." A flip and a turn and Pax had his knee in the attacker's back and the guy's hands tied. Pax dragged the guy to the opposite side of the trash Dumpster and stuffed something in the unconscious man's mouth. "I'm going up."

She was smart enough to know that qualified as a bad idea. "No, Pax. Not without Joel or someone else here to help."

"I sense a lack of trust in my abilities." The scowl had morphed into a determined stare.

She didn't like either look. Not when they led to him walking straight into danger. "We should get out of here for now."

"This isn't a vote." When Joel exhaled into the comm with enough force to make the line crackle, Pax closed his eyes. They had cleared when he opened them again and walked back to her. "This is my job, Kelsey."

"And?"

"Let me protect you."

"I am."

"Good." He winked and then got to her back door. He used the key she'd given him and disappeared up the staircase.

She stammered, choking out a few words before finally getting one out. "Does he always move that fast?"

"You should see him without the injury," Joel said.

"I'm just hoping he doesn't make the leg worse." She really wanted Pax to say something in response, but he'd gone silent on the comm. The longer his silence lasted, the more her worry festered.

She bit her lip as she stared at the closed door. More than anything she wanted to break in and run upstairs just to check on him. To hear him talk. To see him.

"He'll be okay," Joel said as if reading her mind or seeing the concern on her face.

She didn't know which one, but she wanted a guarantee of his assurance. Joel started swearing. Not just a word or two. No, this was a whole line that spelled trouble. "We have a new problem."

"I'd guessed that." The line filled with three long clicks that had Kelsey tapping the mic in her ear. "What was that?"

"A signal for Pax." Joel's breathing grew louder. "Kelsey, you have someone rounding the corner and about to head down the alley in your direction."

Her heart thundered in her ears until everything sounded stuffy and distorted. The sounds of the small city blended into the background as she fell against the wall and struggled to breathe. "It could be someone who works or lives on the street."

"I did the facial recognition scan and it turned up negative."

She shook her head, trying to block out the fear that was

slowly swamping every inch of her body. "You can do that from your desk miles away?"

"Kelsey, I want you to go inside," Joel said.

"And?"

"I'm on the way down." Pax's low voice finally rumbled into the quiet. "Kelsey, move."

Chapter Eight

Pax stopped halfway up the narrow staircase to Kelsey's apartment above the coffee shop when he heard Joel's warning about their new guest. Balancing his hands on the walls that were barely a shoulder width apart, Pax pivoted on his good leg and took the stairs two at a time back to the entry.

As he neared the bottom, the outside door opened and Kelsey slipped inside. With wide eyes and a face paled to a color that almost matched the off-white paint, she stared up at him. She tugged her bottom lip between her teeth and hugged the black T-shirt she'd slipped on before they left the team headquarters.

He would be happy to go a lifetime without seeing that fear on her face again.

Careful not to bang his feet against the steps or make any unnecessary noise, he closed the distance between them, stopping on the step right above her. She didn't say anything. Didn't have to. Her frozen facial features and the subtle tremble moving through her and shaking her shoulders said it all.

Before he could talk through all the cons and argue against the idea, he put his hands on her upper arms. The touch sent a shot of electricity through him. It wasn't until he blinked out the need clouding his brain that the coolness under his palms registered. It had to be eighty degrees outside, but her skin felt as if she'd walked through a gusting fall wind.

She moved in as he bent his head. His lips pressed against her forehead and into her soft hair. The scent of strawberry hit him a second later.

He mumbled against her skin, trying to forget they weren't alone in any sense. "It's going to be okay. I'll get you out of here."

Instead of answering, she nodded and kept doing it as she wrapped her arms around his waist and tucked her head under his chin.

At her touch, his body stiffened. Not that he didn't crave the feel of her but because he'd imagined her like this for weeks, burrowed against him, and the live version blew the fantasy away.

This was the wrong place and about as wrong a time as she could pick. But he let it happen. Closed his eyes for the briefest of moments and fell into the heat that sparked just from holding her close. His shoulders relaxed but the rest of him kicked into gear.

What he wanted with her started with closeness, but it blew way past that fast. He was a normal guy with serious needs. He'd been watching her for weeks, dreaming about her every night since, imagining her in his bed with her clothes on the floor. A minute more of this and it wouldn't matter who stood just outside the door or listened in.

Since he refused to have their first time together happen on a dark staircase with danger lurking nearby, he had to let go. She probably only wanted comfort anyway. A sure arm and a minute to gather her strength. Taking advantage of that, letting his fantasies fuel his actions, made him a complete jerk.

Gritting his teeth and forcing his thoughts away from the softness of her skin and the perfect fit of her body against his, he slipped his hands behind his back and felt for her hands. Bringing them around and trapping them against his chest as he held on, he met her gaze. He saw eyes clear yet wary, but something else lingered there. Determination.

Now there's a good woman.

"We're going to head up to your apartment and call in reinforcements."

She gave him a weak smile. "I like that plan."

That's funny because he hated it, but there was a limit to how much she could take. She wasn't an operative or trained in serious combat. He'd seen hints of a self-defense class graduate, but that didn't mean she could fight a bullet or men twice her size.

He nodded toward the top of the stairs. "Head up."

"Not without you." Her hands clenched against his stomach as she whispered.

They both kept their voices low, barely registering above a hum. "I'm going to be right behind you. I just want to double-check the door lock."

"Pax—"

"You can watch me as you go." He guided her around him. Not an easy task, since only a breath or two separated them already.

"Somebody move," Joel said, breaking through one kind of tension to remind Pax of the one that should be his focus.

Still, Joel's breathing and sarcastic tone didn't kill the mood. Kelsey's body brushed against Pax and his brain caught fire.

Beating back every stupid male thought, he mentally counted to twenty. When that didn't work, he tried it in Spanish. Finally, she stood above him, close enough for him to reach out and touch, but far enough for some of his lost air to rush back into his body.

Pax descended the last three steps and stood at the small foyer leading to the outside. He knew from Kelsey's rundown of the property back at the team house that this door locked automatically. She used the key from the outside to double lock it. From this side it was a matter of throwing the dead bolt.

With a slow, steady turn, being as quiet as he could, he set the top lock. He winced as it caught with a soft click. Later he'd talk with her about a new security system complete with blaring alarms and a direct line to his phone, but right now he wanted the extra insurance the door would hold.

He looked around for reinforcements. There was a hook on the wall and a lock on the door. Neither would keep out a guy determined to bust his way in.

He glanced over his shoulder and saw Kelsey nearing the top of the staircase. She walked with her back skimming the banister against one wall and her gaze trained on him. He nodded to let her know she was doing great.

Any other civilian he knew, except maybe Davis's wife, Lara, would be curled in a ball on the floor. Certainly crying and clinging. Not Kelsey. She fought back and didn't run.

Just when he thought she couldn't get any sexier, she did.

He reached into his back pocket and took out another security tie. He wanted to wedge something under the door, but there was nothing there to work with. That left strengthening the lock's hold.

"How's it coming?"

Pax answered Joel's question with a grunt. It was all he could manage and more than he could afford if he wanted to keep his presence just inside the door hidden.

Without turning the knob, he slipped the tie over the handle and stretched it. The mail slot on the opposite side of the door was his only choice. He worked his finger into the plaster behind one side of the metal rim until he made a small hole. Wedging the thinner end of the tie through the space he made, he shoved and pushed until it came out the other side. He finished it off by looping it around and clicking it into place.

He heard the rustle of clothing and glanced up. Kelsey hadn't moved from her position on the stairs, leaning against the wall. He had to smile at the way she lounged up there, as if being inside with him made her feel safe. She was, just not from him and the need kicking hard against his gut.

He couldn't fight off a smile as his feet fell on the steps with a practiced light touch. The muscles in his right leg had stiffened until bending his knee proved difficult, but nothing was going to stop him from getting up there to her.

They stood a few feet apart with him on the stair below hers. "Let's get in your place so we can put another lock between us and the guy outside."

"Definitely."

Pax tapped the mic to press it snug in his ear after all the up-and-down pounding on the stairs. "Joel, let Connor know we need some help here."

"Already done."

Pax put his hand on Kelsey's lower back and guided her up the remaining steps. There were two doors at the top of the landing. She went to the one with the peephole. He stood in front of the other.

"What's this?" He pointed at the unidentified door.

"Hot water heater."

Sounded small and cramped. Pax nodded and turned away. Then he turned back to it. Closed doors made him twitchy. The entrance to the outside had been locked down with no obvious signs of a break-in. Still, Joel's cameras didn't capture this area, and the in and out of this operation had run smoothly. Well, better than most operations, including the last one, which got him shot.

Kelsey stood with her hand on the doorknob. "Where's the key to my place?"

He slipped it out of his jeans pocket. "I'll open it."

But he couldn't force his body to move or his gaze to meet hers. An ache started at the base of his neck and moved right up to the back of his head. In seconds he went from a vague sense of uneasiness to a pounding in his brain.

Kelsey stepped over and put her hand on his arm. "What's wrong?"

He shook his head. He'd just opened his mouth to respond when the utility door slammed open, right into Pax's head. His neck snapped back and his vision blinked out. A wave of black threatened to swamp him, but Kelsey's sharp intake of breath stopped his downward slide.

She couldn't scream. He couldn't shoot. Not without bringing the guy outside crashing in.

Before his vision refocused, Pax kicked out. A sharp whack followed by the crack of bone. The attacker fell back into the heater. The tank shook and metal clanged against metal as the attacker's gun hit it.

Pax had just enough time to shove Kelsey into the corner and as far away from the fight as possible on the six-by-six landing before taking a punch to his side. He bent double, his free arm moving too late for the block.

"What's happening?" Joel yelled his question into the comm.

"Guest." That was as far as Pax got, all the words he could force out over panting and groaning, before the attacker hit him dead-on.

Head down and shoulder aimed, the guy made a run for Pax's already sore midsection, pounding him against the far wall. Air choked out of Pax's lungs as his right leg slipped underneath him and his gun fell to the floor. He shifted his weight, and the bottom of his shoe hit the edge of the first step. Throwing his body to the opposite side, he put a little distance between him and a serious fall.

He traced his foot over the floor in search for his weapon. He struck something hard and lifted his foot to grab it the best he could, but he hit only carpet. He tapped around and nothing. The gun was gone.

Pax resorted to punching. The attacker huffed and grunted as his stomach weathered the punishing blows. Still, he kept a hold on Pax, shoving him against the wall and screwing the leverage he needed to put his full strength behind the hits.

The attacker let up and then plowed against Pax's stomach even harder a second time. Momentum doubled the pressure and pushed him harder against the wall. Before he could catch his breath, the guy laid his forearm against Pax's throat and pressed.

Pax heard Joel's voice in the distance but couldn't make out the words. Something about being quiet and hitting square. Pax was too busy trying to stay on his feet and not get killed to analyze the words. He needed an opening and fast.

With his jaw locked, the attacker opened his mouth, baring his teeth in a snarl. "I'm done playing with you."

"I'm not stopping you from leaving."

"I'm taking the girl with me."

No way in hell was that happening.

The guy leaned in until his face hovered just inches from Pax's. "Nothing smart to say to that? No comeback?"

Pax said a silent thank-you to the idiot attacker for getting so close. Knowing it would hurt but not having a choice, Pax slammed his forehead into the attacker's nose. There was a crack and a wave of dizziness just before Pax felt something pinch in his neck.

At least he wasn't alone. The attacker reeled back, bringing his empty hand to his face as he let out a battle-cry roar that cut off when Pax punched him in the jaw. When the attacker looked up again, a seething rage filled his eyes.

Pax knew he had seconds only. He shook his head, trying

to fight off the sensation of the room spinning around him. Blinking and stumbling, he scanned the floor for his gun but didn't see it. How was that possible?

Panic clawed at him as he lifted his head, prepared to block the oncoming blow as he made a last grasp for the attacker's weapon. Pax had barely focused on the guy when he saw Kelsey, arm raised and the butt of a gun ready. He couldn't figure out where she got it or where she found the courage to leap in.

Without any hesitation or even a glance in his direction, she brought the weapon down in a slamming arc. Then did it again. The multiple shots did the trick.

The guy's eyes rolled back right before his body went limp. He dropped the gun and followed it to the floor. He hit the landing and bounced off the top step...and kept going. His body rolled, feet slamming into the wall as he picked up speed, until he landed in a heap.

Pax glanced at the lifeless body of the once-fierce attacker. The guy lay in a sprawl on the bottom landing with one leg bent back at an odd angle and his head tucked under his arm in a way that looked unnatural.

Heavy breathing echoed through the small space. It took Pax a second to realize it came from him. He crashed back into the wall and rested his palms on his knees as he inhaled big gulps.

One look at Kelsey and he saw an openmouthed stare. Her focus didn't shift from the sick scene at the bottom of the stairs.

Joel's voice cut through the odd quiet a second later. "Someone talk to me."

"We're okay." Pax slipped his gun out of Kelsey's limp fingers. She didn't try to tighten them or start when he touched her. He knew that was a very bad sign.

Taking the steps two at a time, sliding across the wall to

Ruthless

keep from putting any more weight on his leg, Pax got to the bottom of the stairs. A quick check told him what he already knew. "The guy's dead."

It was rough and messy, but it was over. This round anyway.

"Did she do it?" Joel asked, shock evident in his voice.

There was only one "she" around here. Pax's gaze zipped back to Kelsey. She stared at him with a face tight with stress.

"No, she knocked him out. Looks like the fall is what actually killed him."

"I did it. Oh, my God, it was me." She wrapped her arms around her waist, and her body rocked.

He made his way back up the stairs to stand in front of her. "You stopped the attack. You didn't kill him. Don't take that on."

She nodded but it wasn't convincing. Her gaze bounced off the walls and to the ceiling. Anywhere but to him and the guy at the bottom of the stairs.

He bowed his head until she looked at him again. "That guy picked the location at the top of the stairs. It's not your fault he fell the way he did."

She swallowed several times. "I just did everything he told me."

Pax still had no idea what was happening. "Who?"

"Me. Didn't you hear me calling out directions over the comm?" Joel scoffed. "Not bad for doing it blind, and it sounds like our girl did great."

Pax's mind exploded in fifty different directions. Kelsey saved him. He shook his head as he let that fact sink in.

"Kelsey?" He reached out to her but grabbed only air when she slid down to sit on the top step.

"That was more than I expected. It looks so easy on television. And back at the office? It sounded clear and simple. Go in, get the box and get out." She said the words nice and slow, putting a long pause between each one. "But in real life—"

"I know."

She held out her arm in the direction of the dead man at the bottom of the stairs. "That happens. I didn't expect how it would look or how empty I'd feel. I mean, I get that I didn't have a choice, but…"

She choked and Pax worried she'd throw up. "I'm sorry it was you."

"I'm sorry about all of this."

Pax did an internal assessment and couldn't come up with a body part that didn't ache. From his head to his leg, every muscle begged for a rest. "Makes two of us."

She pulled back her arm and held her hands out in front of her. Turning them over, she studied every inch. They shook hard enough to make the key in her hand jingle. "I…yeah, I kind of need to sit down."

"You already are." He braced his palm against the edge of the landing and sat down hard on the step below her. "You okay?"

"No."

He took her cold hands in his, rubbing them in an attempt to bring life back into her cells. "Breathe."

"I can't remember how."

"Don't talk." He put a hand on her thigh and held it there until she looked at him. "That's it. You're doing great."

She frowned. "How can you say that?"

"I'm witnessing it." Man, she had no idea how amazing she was. She held it all together when it counted. "You rushed in and saved me. You didn't worry about the danger to you, and I'll lecture you about that later when I'm not feeling as grateful, but I gotta tell you not many people have stepped up to rescue me."

It was an odd feeling. He sensed lightness and darkness

moving through him. It was as if his brain couldn't analyze it even as a part of him wanted to smile.

Davis had stepped up for him. The guys on his team and former teammates at the DIA.

But this was different. She didn't have a tie to him, and yet she didn't hesitate. It was heroic and stupid and fierce…and he didn't see how he'd ever build a shield against her now.

"I would do it again." She squeezed his hand hard enough to cut off the blood circulation. "But I have to admit I was scared to death."

"Congratulations, you're human." He'd let her hold him— even strangle the life out of him. Whatever she needed to get through the next few minutes, he'd do.

Without any warning, she switched into hyperdrive. She talked in a rush, her words tripping over each other until he had to strain to separate it all out and understand what she was saying. He leaned in to pick up the harsh whispering.

"—and despite everything, the terror the pain, the panic, all I want to do right now is kiss you, which is totally wrong, and not something I should want."

He sat back, sure he was dreaming because she was saying what he *wanted* to hear not what he ever expected to hear. "What?"

"Crazy, right?" She rubbed her thumb over his palm. "We've known each other for a day, and it's all I can think about right now."

"It's been weeks." He knew the exact number because he'd started measuring his day by the number of times she smiled at him and how she'd make time to talk with him.

Man, he had it bad for her.

She rolled her eyes the same way she did when rude people left her shop and she thought no one was watching. "I agree I knew a version of you for that long. I'm talking about this side of you. Actually, I don't know what I'm talking about since those two parts seem to be merging and my anger at you pretending to be this injured sweet guy is gone."

"Technically, I am injured." And just mentioning it made his thigh thump.

But they had a bigger issue to deal with. His heart took off in a hammering run the second after she said the word "kiss," and the sexy touching only added to his building excitement. Between the near heart-attack beat of anticipation and the pressure pushing against his zipper there was no blood left for his head. "As for the kiss—"

"Forget that."

"Admittedly, your timing on this subject sucks."

She nodded. "It's been that kind of day."

No kidding. "Except for that timing thing, I'm in."

She leaned against him with her head dipping in close. "Are you sure? Because I'm probably going insane."

The more the idea of kissing tumbled around in his head, the more desperate he became to taste her. "It's meant to be."

"My impending insanity?"

"The kiss. We've been circling each other since the first day I walked into the shop."

"How romantic."

This time her smile lit up her face. But he remembered the forced calm and the flash of fear from earlier, and the memory sucked the life right out of him. He knew he had to grab on to his control and stick to his training no matter how his body begged for the opposite result.

He lifted their joined hands and kissed the back of hers. "Can't lie, I've wanted to throw you on that counter since that first morning you handed me a coffee of the day, but that was the wrong time and so is this."

"Who are we kidding?" Her shoulders sagged. "It's adrenaline. We'll get over it."

She definitely didn't understand some very important facts

about him. But she would. "Yeah, I'm not likely to let that happen."

"You kiss all the people you protect?"

How she missed the signs and threw herself into the category of the easily forgotten or just like every other woman was a mystery to him. Time for a wake-up call. "You'll be the first, but later, when I can really concentrate on the task."

A forced cough crackled over the comm. "Do I get to listen in then, too?"

Pax wanted to curse, but he had no one to blame but himself for this one. "Joel, I swear I—"

"Okay, kids. Let's finish this job before we start celebrating."

Kelsey held a hand over her mouth. This time her wide-eyed stare had nothing to do with fear. "For a second I forgot he was there."

Joel chuckled directly into their ears. "I love hearing that. You'd be amazed what I pick up from back here."

Gathering all of his concentration and dropping her hand, Pax got back to the operation. It was either that or risk both of their lives on a simple box retrieval. "What about the company in the street?"

"Still there. He's down the alley a bit and pacing."

"What does that mean?" she asked.

The tapping of the keyboard served as background noise to Joel's side of the conversation. "No idea but even with Connor on the way, the quicker you two finish whatever it is you're doing, the better off we'll all be."

She exhaled as she stood up and held out a hand to Pax to have him join her. "You heard the man. Let's get this done."

Chapter Nine

A knock sounded at Bryce's office door. At this time of night, hours after most of the staff went home and the nightly cleaning crew moved in, his visitor could be only one person. At least it was someone he could tolerate for more than a few minutes at a time.

"Come in," he said without taking his attention away from the computer programs running on the monitors.

The door opened a fraction, and Glenn stuck his head inside. "Sir? Did you need anything before I leave for the day?"

The man was loyal to the end. He'd grabbed his briefcase two hours ago in a rush to get to a dinner date and then dropped it again when Bryce announced he was staying to look deeper into the Sean Moore situation. Glenn mumbled something about canceling and sticking around. Soon after that takeout food containers appeared on Bryce's desk and files were placed on the edge of his desk. He combed through it all, reviewing Glenn's report on Sean Moore, including a list of places to look for him.

Glenn produced good work. Some holes existed, but Bryce filled those in on his own. He went beyond the paperwork and the investigator's report. He knew where Sean wasn't at the moment and how few resources he had. That meant the young man would be feeling desperate soon.

Having gone to expensive prep schools and lived in Daddy's gated mansion for most of his life meant Sean's survival skills were likely pretty limited. He didn't have a web of friends or a stash of secret cash. Like many people he depended on a base level of intelligence and comfort to get by, and when something shook the latter the former suffered.

Sean would make a mistake. It was just a matter of time. Bryce just had to wait and find the right way in, which led him to an area in which he was an expert. Electronic surveillance. If Sean so much as burped in the D.C. metro area, Bryce should be able to hunt him down.

For extra insurance, Bryce put behind-the-scenes pressure on Sean's family, which consisted of a half sister and his infamous father. Neither had been contacted by Sean through any of the usual channels Bryce now monitored. He used strategically placed cameras to be ready if Sean found another way.

Which uncovered this evening's most interesting piece of information. Not that Bryce had figured out the connections. It would all be in the details. He needed to gather those.

He glanced at the program running on his main computer. Photos of faces raced by as the program searched for an identity match. But maybe there was an easier way. Maybe Glenn could offer some insight, see something Bryce missed since Glenn spent more time on the floor and dealing directly with employees.

Reality was Bryce made it a priority to know every face in the building. He didn't hire them all, but he had a sense of who should be here and who shouldn't. But the man he was trying to identify could be tangentially related to Kingston or someone who worked there—possibly a delivery guy or someone in the building or associated with a competitor— and Bryce might miss the connection.

He sat back in his chair and pointed at the large computer monitor on the credenza perpendicular to his desk. "Do you have any idea who this is?"

Glenn frowned as he stepped farther into the room. "What are you looking at?"

"Footage."

Glenn's hand tightened around the notepad in his hand. "Of what?"

"Private citizens walking around."

"Excuse me, sir?"

Bryce hoped Glenn didn't bring up a lecture on the web of privacy laws that added unnecessary jumps to simple searches but also made Bryce a great deal of money by defeating those barriers...for the right price, of course. "It's the camera in front of that coffee place Sean's sister runs."

"Owns."

That grabbed Bryce's attention. "What?"

Glenn waved his hand in the air as he continued to stare at the screen. "She owns it."

"I don't care whose name is on the deed." Bryce barely cared about Sean, and that disdain was quickly spreading to his family. From what Bryce could tell, none of them had managed to amount to much of anything, and Sean blew the one chance he had of making a future for himself. "This footage is from more than a half hour ago."

"We have a camera outside of her shop?"

"We have cameras everywhere." A satellite system saw to that. So did the network of police and security cameras Bryce set up throughout the entire region thanks to low job bids he instinctively knew would serve him well in the future. Where he didn't have eyes, he could usually hook into someone else's system and take a look around.

The back door he kept open for his continued use on the systems he designed paid off now. Even now he reversed and fast-forwarded to find the exact frame he needed.

Glenn dropped into the seat across the desk and studied the footage. "I had no idea."

"That's the point." Figures moved across the screen and Bryce stopped the picture on an outline of two people walking down the street, stopping and then turning back again. It was the turn that gave him their faces. He tapped a key to zoom in. "There. The woman is Kelsey Moore or someone who looks a great deal like her. Who's the man?"

"I don't know."

"Here. This will help." With a few more keystrokes Bryce clarified the photo and cropped it to highlight the man's face. "I'm running the facial recognition software but no hits yet."

"Never seen him."

"Think about it. Has he been in the building or with Sean or any other employee?"

Glenn's eyes narrowed. "Not that I know of. What are you thinking about this guy?"

"Sean answers to someone. He's not smart enough, or dumb enough, depending on how you look at it, to pull off this information dump on his own. He knows his way around computers, but we have checks and fail-safes. He bucked them all until he got to the lie detector test. I found the rest when I backtracked after that, but he would have gotten away with it, at least for a while." A fact that continued to burn through Bryce every minute of the day.

Thanks to Sean and his betrayal, Bryce got stuck dealing with people like Dan. Sean would pay for that when Bryce made him pay for everything else.

"And you think the guy on the screen is the person who helped Sean steal data?" Glenn asked.

"I think Sean is looking for a big check, and this man might be the one writing it." Someone pulled the strings. The person at the head of this thing wanted money or propriety software or highly sensitive passwords, or all of it.

"But why would someone involve Sean's sister?"

A simple question. One Bryce found beneath Glenn's skill

set, and he scowled to make his position clear. "Why not? We have."

"True." Glen straightened. "I can check into it."

"No need." This project Bryce needed to handle on his own. He'd delegated too much responsibility, and now he had a personnel disaster that could blow into something much bigger. After he cleared out the employees who failed him, he would impose stricter rules to ensure a security breach like this never happened again. "We'll let the computers do the work for a few hours. If this program doesn't work, I may need to call in some favors and access a more intricate system."

"You're talking about something like at the NSA or CIA?"

Bryce would do whatever it took to secure his company's future. He'd worked too hard for too long, balancing his father-in-law's expectations and risking his wife's wrath to gain a solid reputation and foothold in the market. He would not go backward now. "You can go home."

Glenn's gaze bounced from screen to screen. "If it's okay with you, I'd prefer to stay."

Bryce thought about Dan and his threats. He was the type of employee Bryce didn't need. But Glenn, he was starting to prove himself very capable. "Take a seat."

KELSEY HAD BEEN AWAY from her apartment for exactly one afternoon, but it dragged on as if it were months. She opened the door, expecting the dank scent of the apartment being closed up all day in the humid weather to hit her. Instead, everything looked and smelled normal.

Well, what she saw of it. Pax pushed her into the hallway and put a finger over his lips. The same lips she came within inches of kissing. Yeah, talk about a dumb idea. The man was her assigned bodyguard and even now stalked around her shadowed apartment with his gun up and his attention trained on every corner.

The only light came from a small lamp on an end table. She left it on whenever she was out. Now it shone a soft yellow glow over everything. She reached for the light switch, but his finger snapping stopped her. So did the curt nod of his head.

She'd never been a fan of overly commanding men. She generally associated the trait with the jerky-male type. Those guys who insisted everything be done as they wanted it and slipped into rage-fueled, sometimes abusive fits when things moved off plan. She wondered now if that assessment had been too harsh or at least too general.

When Pax wanted something, he sure didn't have any trouble being bossy to get his way. She should hate that, be on her guard, but from him it calmed her frayed nerves. Sure, sometimes she pushed back or wanted to roll her eyes, but she instinctively knew he'd accept either reaction.

Trust didn't come easy for her, and it should be impossible with Pax in light of how they met, but the opposite proved true.

Even when he acted in a way she didn't understand. Like now. He opened closet doors and ducked to check under furniture. The same furniture that likely served as home to dust bunny families because she sure never checked under there.

When he ducked into the bedroom, she had to fight the urge to follow him in there and check for underwear all over the floor. She wasn't exactly expecting company, after all.

A minute later he stepped back into the family room. This time his arm hung at his side and his gun didn't point at anything or anybody. "All clear."

Her heart clunked as it fell an inch. "Did you think someone would be up here?"

"Let's just say after the day we've had, I'm not taking any

chances. That includes keeping the lights off so we don't draw attention to your place."

Since she was admittedly a below-average housekeeper, it probably looked better in the dark anyway. She tried to see the place through his eyes. To her, the exposed redbrick walls and bunches of plants near the front window were charming.

The open floor plan appealed to her. Standing at the door she could see the family room with the sectional she found on sale last year and the kitchen stretching along the wall off to her right. Only the bedroom and a small bath were tucked away from immediate view.

The whole space took up less than half of the first floor of the Corcoran place. It was small and cozy and all hers… hers and the bank's. Mostly the bank's.

He glanced around. "The box?"

She dropped the keys on the small table next to the door. "The kitchen."

Pax spun around until he faced the breakfast bar on the family room side of the butcher block island. "You eat with the box? Is that some sort of woman thing I don't know about?"

"I eat with the television. When the workday is over I want mindless entertainment." She pointed at the couch and the flat-screen hooked to the wall. "And I engage in said laziness right there."

That sexy smile appeared out of nowhere. "I approve of that arrangement. Have been known to engage in the same now and then."

She couldn't imagine him ever being lazy. "Just you and your gun, huh?"

"I'd rather try your couch and skip the gun."

She chalked it up to the leftover adrenaline and the fact they stood in the middle of the most private part of her life, but all she wanted was to climb onto the couch and drag Pax there beside her. "Maybe I'll show you sometime."

"At breakfast?" He picked up the box. It was one of those Priority Mail kind you could stuff full and still pay only a set fee. "Once all of this is over and you're safe, if you invite me, I guarantee I'll be here."

"Uh, folks? I'm still listening in," Joel said in a monotone, almost bored voice.

Pax winked at her. "As if we could forget you."

"I'm not the only one you should be worried about," Joel said. "Alley guy is on the move."

Pax's smile disappeared as quickly as it came. "Unbelievable."

She didn't know why he was surprised. Luck had failed them at every turn today. "We can't catch a break here."

"If he's the partner of the one at the bottom of the staircase or the one you stuffed in the corner by the Dumpster, he's probably getting antsy and looking around," Joel said.

Pax tucked the box under his arm. "How close?"

"Right at the outside door downstairs. He keeps looking around and checking the lock. Tugging on it."

Hope flickered to life in her belly. "Good thing Pax fixed it."

"Not to scare you, but if the guy wants in, he'll get in. That's the dirty secret the security companies don't like to admit." Pax's gaze fell on her phone on top of the bar. He held it up. "Your cell?"

What, did he think she had a boyfriend on the side and he dropped it there? "Of course."

"Password-protected?"

She shook her head. It never dawned on her to lock her phone. Half the time she forgot to carry it, which explained why it was up here instead of downstairs in her office or in her back pocket, which would have been a help any one of the times she'd been attacked.

"Speaking of interesting security choices." He tapped a few buttons before his gaze flew back to meet hers. "I don't see anything on here from your brother."

The words slammed into her, pushing her back against the wall. Her mind went blank but her legs suddenly weighed a thousand pounds each. "What does that mean?"

Pax slipped the cell into his jeans pocket. He wore a frown and wasn't paying any attention to her. "I'm not sure yet. I'd just think your brother would call. I mean, how many people can he depend on?"

She wasn't convinced Sean thought of her in those terms, but still…

"Remember our conversation about comfort and how you sort of stink at it? This right here, Pax?" She moved her hands around in small circles. "This is a good example of that."

His head popped up and his eyes narrowed as he focused on her face. "I figured you'd appreciate the honesty."

"Turn off the GPS on that phone and bring it with you," Joel said.

"Got it. Did the same on the attacker's phone earlier." Pax blew out a long breath. "Okay, Joel. How much time do we have?"

"Minutes only."

She tried to think about what she needed. Clothes and some paperwork. She had some cash in her checkbook…oh, and her actual checkbook. Not that there was much in there. "I have to pack a bag."

Pax spared her another glance as he checked the lamp shades and behind a picture frame on the wall of the family room. "Not necessary."

"Maybe to you, but—"

Pax held the mic closer to his ear. "What's Connor's ETA?"

"Almost there. He's breaking away from a conversation with the coroner and should be on the line any second."

Her stomach rolled. Actually disconnected and did a full flip. "I think I'm going to be sick."

He stepped in front of her. "I made you a promise, and I plan to keep it."

"To join me for breakfast?"

"Oh, that's absolutely happening as soon as I can manage it, but I meant about your safety." His palm cupped her cheek. "You're going to be fine."

Before she could answer or even close her eyes and hope he would finally lean in and give her that kiss he'd been promising, Joel broke in on the line. "The guy's really working the lock downstairs. I'd be ready for company any second."

Pax dropped the box on the couch and then reached for his gun. "Resourceful, isn't he?"

Violence wasn't her thing. After a disgruntled employee of her father's kidnapped her all those years ago and demanded her father return a retirement account, she stayed away from scary movies and anything with a lot of bloodshed. The sight of either brought the memories rushing back.

Evan Klinger didn't follow through with the quick death he promised, but the twinges of fear never really went away. She could feel his breath brush over her ear and smell the alcohol on his breath.

And after law enforcement burst in, she could see nothing but Klinger's head as it exploded from the rounds of gunfire. The paper said he "went down in a hail of bullets." If she closed her eyes the headline screamed across her senses.

Despite everything she'd gone through that weekend long ago, or maybe because of it, she always thought she'd be the

last person to pull a trigger. Now she knew differently. She'd
already used one end as a weapon. She wouldn't hesitate to
use the fatal end, either.

"Shoot him if you have to," she said.

"I like her style." She could hear the smile in Joel's voice
as he said the words.

"You stay here." Pax talked right over her when she started
to argue. "I'm not going to worry about where you're standing during a shoot-out. Understand?"

"That goes both ways." The idea of him getting hurt nearly
doubled her over. She thought about his leg and a guilt-edged
sadness filled her. If she were the reason for another injury,
if he sacrificed his life for hers… Her mind closed down at
the thought.

Pax held up his gun. "You forget I have the upper hand."

She could think of a couple of advantages he had over
every man she'd ever known. "You mean Secret Weapon
Joel?"

He laughed. "Thanks for the vote of confidence."

Pax pressed his finger against the door. "The peephole. I
can see the bad guys coming."

"I wish I were as positive about this as you are."

"Go stand at the entrance to the bedroom. Listen to Joel
and do not come out unless I tell you it's okay." When she
tried to protest, he put a finger over her lips. "I need you here,
safe and where I can sort of see you. Anything else will dis-
tract me and put us both in danger. Now, I'll ask again. Do
you understand?"

She nodded because she didn't trust her voice to speak.

His thumb brushed across her bottom lip before his hand
dropped. After one last smile he turned back to the door
and she headed to the wall separating the bedroom hallway
from the rest of the space. She could hear him whispering

but didn't know what he was saying. For some reason the comm in her ear went deathly silent.

Pax stopped at the door. "Joel?"

A quiet buzz filled the line. Pax glanced at her and she shook her head. She couldn't pick up anything and from the way all emotion wiped clear of his face, she guessed he couldn't, either.

He pointed toward the kitchen. Since he seemed to know something she didn't, and whatever it was had his face flushing and his eyes snapping with fury, she followed his direction. She bent down and made a determined rush for the island that separated the kitchen from the rest of the apartment.

Peeking from behind it, she saw him hold out his hand and press it palm down, which she took as a signal for her to drop. She did, scraping her knee as she went. Her butt hit the floor and she shifted to her knees before glancing up again. She hugged the corner and watched.

He stood next to the door rather than right behind it. From that spot there was no way he could see out the peephole. She didn't understand how he could even turn the knob from that awkward position.

He motioned for her to bend down even lower and cover her head. She was about to do that when he reached over and flicked the knob.

The door flew open and bounced against the opposite wall. Gunfire boomed a second later. A rapid succession of five shots had plaster kicking up. The wood on the door splintered and a glass shattered somewhere off to her right. She stayed tucked but peeked up in time to see Pax shift around the corner of the open doorway. One shot and a series of thuds. Then silence.

He darted out of the room and footsteps echoed on the landing. She couldn't wait one more second to see what happened. She got up, slipping around the outside of the room and sticking to the walls. When she looked out the door, she saw Pax bending over a still body sprawled at the top of the stairs. Blood splattered against the wall and spread in a dark circle on the downed guy's forehead.

Pax slipped a gun into the back of his jeans and conducted another pat down. One more cell appeared before he pocketed it. After all the work, he looked up at her. "You okay?" He wasn't even out of breath.

"You got him."

"We were lucky he fell for the subterfuge." Pax looked at her and then down at the obviously dead body. "Don't look at him."

"That's kind of hard."

Pax tapped his ear and called for Joel, but the line stayed silent. "It was him or us, Kelsey. These guys aren't giving us options."

"I get that." If someone had told her this morning that she'd be dealing with dead bodies and a shoot-out in addition to the pastry inventory, she would have passed out. Somehow living through it, surviving and staying on her feet even though danger lurked in every hallway filled her with a strength and fearlessness she always wished she'd had. *Definitely some weird sort of adrenaline rush.*

While Pax moved around with an almost scary level of detached efficiency, she put the puzzle pieces of the past few minutes together in her mind. "You wanted him to fire first."

"It gave away his exact location." Pax stood up.

She did a visual search of his body. There were no signs that one of those bullets hit him. Relieved, she sagged against the doorjamb and let her gaze linger over her apartment. It had not fared as well.

She spied a ripped sofa cushion and shards of glass from the picture frame sprayed over everything. There was a hole in her door and an odd gash in her brick wall by the television. Her perfect place of solace, the one spot she could go to relax and unwind, had been violated in a way that had her stomach dropping to her feet.

She couldn't deal with that right now. "I'm ready to leave."

Then he was there. She turned her head and his face hovered over hers. One hand balanced above her and he leaned in close. "Any chance you're also ready for that kiss?"

"I kind of feel like I could throw up."

He stepped back. "So, we'll go with later on the kiss then."

He didn't get it. How could he, because she could barely accept it enough to talk about it. Still, she had to try. "People depend on me. I have a mortgage and a business loan. I can't be closed, but I can't put people in danger, either."

"Hold up for a second and listen to me." He rested his hands on her hips and held her still. "You still need to breathe."

"Right." She nodded but the whole air thing wasn't happening.

He rubbed her arm, caressed her face. With gentle touches and a soft voice he brought her back from the brink of a full-on emotional breakdown. Her emotions whipped between fury at her brother for putting her in this position and a sick dizziness as the smell of blood and mix of sulfur hit her senses.

But when he stood there, so close, wooing her back from the edge, she grabbed on to the mental lifeline.

"We're going to fix this and you're going to reopen, and I'll buy enough coffee to make up for a day or two of being closed." His fingers trailed along the line of her chin.

Everything he said turned the thunder of terror into a soft ripple. "You're sweet."

"Not really." His thumb traveled across her lips. "My point is it's going to be okay."

She lost herself in the sensation of his touch. "How do you know?"

"Because I'm guaranteeing it."

"And you're a man of your word." It wasn't a question, because she knew the answer.

"Exactly."

"You may just get that kiss later after all." She almost didn't recognize her breathy voice, but she understood the rapid tapping of her heart.

The door at the bottom of the stairs shot open, and a man jumped into the space.

Pax shoved her behind him and aimed his gun. Tension vibrated off him and smacked against the walls of the small space. But as quickly as it came the stiffness left his shoulders. He held up his hand. "Whoa. It's us."

The fear clogging her senses eased, and she focused on the guy aiming the gun at them from below. Connor. He dropped his weapon, but the frown didn't let up. "What the hell happened in here?"

Pax shifted his weight and brought her to his side. "You didn't hear the fight?"

"My comm went cold. Couldn't pick up anything until a second ago." Connor gave the explanation, but Kelsey would have answered the same way.

Pax swore under his breath. "Nice work, Joel."

"I wasn't me." Joel bust on the comm with the usual tapping sound in the background. "Well, it was. Sort of."

"What does all of that mean?" Connor asked after a healthy string of profanity of his own.

"Someone was piggybacking my signal. I killed it to keep them from listening in, just in case the attackers were monitoring your positions."

The bad news just kept coming, and Kelsey barely understood this part. "Wait a second—"

Joel rushed over top of her comment. "But whoever it was is skilled. They blocked all other signals. I had to switch to a backup to stay on you guys."

Pax's mouth dropped. "You waited until now to tell us all of this?"

"Hey, knowing a few minutes ago only would have made you panic."

"I'm not sure how I feel about that answer." She mumbled the response but Connor nodded in agreement.

"My point is, the person who crashed our party has the kind of equipment we do."

At Joel's comment, she opened her eyes again.

Pax glanced down at Connor. "I thought we had government-grade, top-of-the-line stuff."

Connor was staring right at her. "Looks like there's a big player in this thing, and your brother is getting that person's attention."

"Didn't we already know that?" She glanced between Pax and Connor. "I mean, someone in the government hired you guys. Who was that, by the way?"

"I'm not sure how you know all that, but yes," Connor said. "Someone at the Department of Defense called us in."

Pax piped up. "And now we know why."

Maybe they did. She didn't. "We do?"

"Your brother didn't just take some information. It's very possible he's planning on selling it." Connor put his gun away. "If so, this game just got a whole lot more dangerous."

With the way her body started shutting down, every inch falling into a fatigue-hued exhaustion, she doubted she'd be on her feet much longer even if she skipped asking. So she went ahead and asked. "Why?"

"Honestly?" Joel's deep voice cut through the sudden silence. "Because Sean's playmates won't stop until they kill him."

Chapter Ten

It was almost midnight when Bryce rubbed his blurry eyes and read the last line in the stacks of compiled information about Sean Moore. For a twenty-something, there seemed to be a lot of paperwork on the kid. No wonder his security clearance took longer than expected.

Probably also had something to do with attending three colleges, getting kicked out of two and having a father who'd spent time in jail for bilking people. The same father who had two children from two different wives, and both wives were dead.

It was quite a life story.

Sean's mother died in a car accident when Sean hit nineteen and the sister, well…Bryce still couldn't figure out where she fit in. There wasn't so much as a photo with them together. She lost her mother to cancer and then her father did a family-restart and Sean was the result.

Now it looked as if he'd been the wrong kid to hire, but he'd possessed very specific math skills described as "off the charts" by more than one reference. Human resources pushed for him to be added to the team, something about him being a near-perfect candidate in terms of aptitude.

Bryce did a cursory sign-off because the idea of a loner who needed a second chance sounded like a familiar story. It appealed to him as a way to breed loyalty. His uncle had once given him a similar chance, and Bryce ran with it. Clearly, history did not repeat itself with Sean.

Lesson learned.

Bryce lifted his head and rubbed his aching neck. The stiffness had traveled over his shoulders and down to his lower back. But he couldn't let up. Sean was a loose end Bryce needed tied up.

Being in a position where someone like Dan had the upper hand made Bryce furious. His business plan centered on using Dan's history to Kingston's benefit and otherwise ignoring the man. Having it work any other way was absolutely unacceptable.

Bryce shook his head, and a single light shining in the area just outside of his office door caught his attention. The floor was dark but Glenn hadn't gone home. Since he hadn't made a noise in over thirty minutes, Bryce wondered if the younger man had dropped off.

Bryce eyed the empty coffee carafe before his gaze went to the computer screen. The photos had stopped flipping by, meaning the program had found a match.

He pulled his chair up tight against his desk, hearing the wheels creak underneath him as he read the information on the screen, limited as it was.

Paxton Weeks. That was it. A name, a photo and a black bar marked Confidential.

Bryce fell back in his plush chair. He felt nothing except the rush of air moving in and out as his breathing picked up its pace.

The notation could indicate many things, but it did suggest Sean and his sister weren't regular citizens scrambling to get by. This Paxton Weeks character was highly connected, which meant Sean knew powerful people. Potentially dangerous people.

People who could ruin Kingston without providing Bryce an opportunity to salvage anything.

The game had just changed. Dan and Sean were no longer Bryce's biggest headaches. This Paxton Weeks guy was.

PAX SAT AT the conference room table back at team headquarters. He'd showered and changed and managed to chug back two cups of coffee. Not that he needed the caffeine. Adrenaline powered him now. That and painkillers. If he took one more tablet he might kill some brain cells along with the residual thumping in his leg.

The idea turned out to be more of a temptation than Pax expected. Something about Kelsey being in danger kept him on edge. Even now he wanted to grab her up and take her far from there until all signs of trouble disappeared.

She sat across from him, tapping her fingernails on the box they'd picked up at her house and staring at it while she chomped on her bottom lip. With her damp hair pulled up in a ponytail and her face scrubbed clean, she swiveled her chair from side to side.

The outfit she'd put on was giving him fits. The V-neck shirt looked about a size too big. It kept falling off her shoulder, revealing a thin strip of a bra strap. She even managed to make oversized navy sweatpants look sexy.

The woman was killing the last hold on his control. To get his mind back on the job, he focused on Connor. The leader paced the space behind Kelsey's chair.

"Where's Ben?" Pax asked.

Kelsey edged her nail along the seam of the box. "I'm starting to think this guy doesn't exist. I hear about this Ben person but have never seen him. Call me skeptical."

The joking comment helped Pax find his first smile in hours. "He'll love knowing you think he's fictional."

"At least she thinks about him. That's something," Joel said and then turned back to the computer when Pax glared.

"Ben is at the hospital." Connor continued his trek over the carpet as he stared at his feet and drank his coffee. "He's had trouble."

Joel's head shot up again. "What does that mean?"

"Someone came after the comatose bad guy, which suggests whoever paid him to kidnap Kelsey doesn't want him waking up and talking."

Pax nodded.

"Ben figured out the situation and diffused it, but the attacker got away." Connor exhaled. "Apparently, Ben didn't want to shoot around all the sick people."

"Good call." Pax could imagine the whole thing and how Ben, the former NCIS agent and straightest arrow of them all, must have hated missing his target.

For Ben's sake, Pax hoped there was a good-looking nurse on the floor to ease Ben's pain.

Kelsey frowned. "These people after Sean, whoever they are, are now causing trouble in hospitals? What kind of person risks the lives of innocent people like that?"

She missed a pretty important piece of the puzzle. Pax didn't. "You're innocent and they came after you."

"Yeah, these are the kind of folks you don't want to meet in an alley behind your shop," Joel said.

Pax knew the real answer was so much worse than Joel's light tone suggested. People like this—hired killers, mercenaries without any loyalty—crawled out from under many rocks and worked for the highest bidder. It was a lousy way to make a living but pretty lucrative.

Even though he wanted her to feel secure and ease up on the killer clench of her fingers into fists, he needed her to be careful. "These men? They'll do anything to get what they want."

FREE Merchandise is 'in the Cards' for you!

Dear Reader,

We're giving away FREE MERCHANDISE!

Seriously, we'd like to reward you for reading this novel by giving you **FREE MERCHANDISE** worth over $20. And no purchase is necessary!

You see the Jack of Hearts sticker above? Paste that sticker in the box on the Free Merchandise Voucher inside. Return the Voucher promptly...and we'll send you valuable Free Merchandise!

Thanks again for reading one of our novels—and enjoy your Free Merchandise with our compliments!

Pam Powers

Pam Powers

P.S. Look inside to see what Free Merchandise is **"in the cards"** for you!

HI-FM-08/13

We'd like to send you two free books to introduce you to the Harlequin Intrigue® series. These books are worth over $10, but they are yours to keep absolutely FREE! We'll even send you 2 wonderful surprise gifts. You can't lose!

REMEMBER: Your Free Merchandise, consisting of **2 Free Books** and **2 Free Gifts**, is worth over $20.00! No purchase is necessary, so please send for your Free Merchandise today.

Plus TWO FREE GIFTS!

We'll also send you two wonderful FREE GIFTS (worth about $10), in addition to your 2 Free Harlequin Intrigue books!

Visit us at:

www.ReaderService.com

YOUR FREE MERCHANDISE INCLUDES...
2 FREE Harlequin Intrigue® Books
AND 2 FREE Mystery Gifts

FREE MERCHANDISE VOUCHER

2 FREE
BOOKS
and
2 FREE
GIFTS

Please send my Free Merchandise, consisting of
2 Free Books and **2 Free Mystery Gifts**.
I understand that I am under no obligation to buy
anything, as explained on the back of this card.

❏ I prefer the regular-print edition   ❏ I prefer the larger-print edition
182/382 HDL F4ZP   199/399 HDL F4ZP

Please Print

FIRST NAME

LAST NAME

ADDRESS

APT.#   CITY

STATE/PROV.   ZIP/POSTAL CODE

NO PURCHASE NECESSARY!

HARLEQUIN® READER SERVICE—**Here's How It Works:**

Accepting your 2 free books and 2 free gifts (gifts valued at approximately $10.00) places you under no obligation to buy anything. You may keep the books and gifts and return the shipping statement marked "cancel." If you do not cancel, about a month later we'll send you 6 additional books and bill you just $4.74 each for the regular-print edition or $5.49 each for the larger-print edition in the U.S. or $5.24 each for the regular-print edition or $5.99 each for the larger-print edition in Canada. That is a savings of at least 13% off the cover price. It's quite a bargain! Shipping and handling is just 50¢ per book in the U.S. and 75¢ per book in Canada.* You may cancel at any time, but if you choose to continue, every month we'll send you 6 more books, which you may either purchase at the discount price or return to us and cancel your subscription.

*Terms and prices subject to change without notice. Prices do not include applicable taxes. Sales tax applicable in N.Y. Canadian residents will be charged applicable taxes. Offer not valid in Quebec. Books received may not be as shown. All orders subject to credit approval. Credit or debit balances in a customer's account(s) may be offset by any other outstanding balance owed by or to the customer. Please allow 4 to 6 weeks for delivery. Offer available while quantities last.

◀ If offer card is missing write to: Harlequin Reader Service, P.O. Box 1867, Buffalo, NY 14240-1867 or visit www.ReaderService.com ▶

BUSINESS REPLY MAIL

FIRST-CLASS MAIL   PERMIT NO. 717   BUFFALO, NY

POSTAGE WILL BE PAID BY ADDRESSEE

HARLEQUIN READER SERVICE

PO BOX 1867

BUFFALO NY 14240-9952

NO POSTAGE
NECESSARY
IF MAILED
IN THE
UNITED STATES

"Which is? I'm still not completely clear on that," she said.

Connor reached over her shoulder and flattened his hand against the mysterious box. "This might give us an idea."

It was time. They'd stalled long enough, trying to take fifteen minutes away from the draining case to clean up and recharge, but they couldn't put off looking. All the coffee and small talk in the world could do only so much to battle the anticipation that had them all twitching.

If Joel shifted one more time he might accidentally unplug a computer. And Connor, well, his feet fell harder and faster with each pacing pass.

As much as Pax wanted to rip into the box and get on with it, the right to open it belonged to Kelsey. He held out a hand. "Go ahead."

She glanced around the room at all of them before nodding. Without saying anything, she picked it up and put it on her lap. She picked at the tab and carefully ripped it open.

That had to be one of the differences between men and women. Pax knew he would have torn it apart with his bare hands and dumped everything out in less than five seconds. They'd already be searching through the contents for a lead.

But not Kelsey. She opened it as if it were the most precious gift.

Even with the longer route she finally got there and dumped it upside down. Papers spilled across the table and something clicked as it performed an awkward roll. A smack of her hand stopped it.

She gathered everything in her arms and read off an informal inventory. "Memory stick, a stack of papers written in some weird code and copies of some documents."

Connor reached over her shoulder again, this time to page through the papers strewn in front of her. He separated a stack and held them up. "Some of this looks like a job for Joel."

"Your temporary tech expert is happy to be at your service." Joel's chair creaked as he wheeled it closer to the table.

Connor shot Joel a one-eyed scowl. "You could get up, you know."

"I'm good here."

Her hands froze. "Temporary?"

Joel took what looked like a ream of papers from Connor. "I'm a gun guy filling in as a computer nerd while our regular nerd is with the other part of the team in Catalina."

"Whoa." Kelsey lifted out of her chair and smacked her hand against the papers before Joel could drag them away. Even ignored his "hey" of outrage. "Gentlemen, before you go running in different directions and talking in annoying half sentences, please fill in the newbie. We're not doing the confuse-the-nonoperative game anymore. From here on in, I'm one of you, only without the shooting skills."

Connor's eyebrow lifted. "Excuse me?"

She didn't roll her eyes, but she sure looked as if she wanted to. "Don't bother with the I'm-in-charge voice." She threw her arms out wide. "Tell me what all of this is."

Pax didn't bother to hide his smile. Seeing the matching stunned expressions on Joel's and Connor's faces pretty much made Pax's horrible day take a left turn into more tolerable territory.

They were friends as well as teammates. From watching them interact with Lara and seeing Connor with his wife, Jana, though that had been awhile, Pax didn't doubt his friends' appreciation of strong women.

Erica Dane had been on the team for almost a year and no one treated her as an afterthought. Probably because her sniper skills rivaled Connor's. But with Erica on consecutive out-of-country jobs, Lara on her honeymoon with Davis and Jana inexplicably away, there had been little female input lately. Having Kelsey step up and make a claim seemed to throw Connor off, and to a lesser extent Joel.

It wasn't often a potential victim wandered into the tactical end of the business. They were used to finding a clue, picking it apart and then establishing a plan.

Having Kelsey, the person they viewed as the subject of their operation, make a demand stopped their momentum. She didn't blindly accept everything happening around her and beg for help when things blew up. She asked questions.

Pax took it as a sign they needed more women on the team. He'd be fine if they started with Kelsey, so long as she never left the desk and hypersecure space patrolled by armed guards. He decided that was a totally logical requirement, since he'd reached his end on seeing her in danger.

Before the room exploded in questions or anything else, Pax reached into the not-quite-empty box and pulled out a slip of paper. The temptation to read it proved great, but he slid it in front of Kelsey. "Here."

"A note?" She turned it over in her hands and then read it. A deep exhale followed a second later. "Leave it to Sean to push up the drama with a cryptic letter. The only letter, email, card or even sticky note he's ever written to me, by the way."

"What does it say?" Connor asked.

"Not much. 'Hold these for me—I'll explain later' and that's it." She handed it to Connor. "No explanation."

That's not what ticked Pax off. "No apology."

"I didn't expect one." She smiled but the expression didn't hide the sad note in her voice.

With that, the brief window of amusement Pax had been enjoying slammed shut. He shot out of his chair and did some pacing of his own on this side of the table. "What the hell is wrong with your brother? He put you in the middle of this mess and doesn't bother to warn you or make sure you're okay."

"I doubt he cares." Kelsey divided up the contents of the box. Connor got the documents. Joel got the readouts and memory stick. She held on to the note and likely didn't realize she traced the words with her finger. "We weren't—"

"Close. Yeah, I got that the first few times you said it. It's burned in my brain at this point, not that I need the reminder. Your brother's actions speak loud enough." Pax tried to shake off the frustration bouncing through him. The idea her family would dump her into danger and then run off and leave her to handle it sent a spike of white-hot rage shooting to his brain.

He paced and swore under his breath. It took him another few minutes to realize he was the only one making any noise. He felt the attention on him and looked up to find three sets of eyes focused on him. "What?"

"Something else you want to say about my family?" she asked in a soft voice.

He knew that expression. He could spot a furious female within a hundred feet, and this one looked ready to burst into flames. And not in a good way.

He did what any smart person would do. Stayed as still and quiet as possible. "No."

She stood up, almost in slow motion, but something about the force of the move had her chair spinning behind her. She balanced her palms against the table. "I know we're not perfect. We might even be the lead example for dysfunctional."

"That's not up for debate, but I'm talking about Sean's behavior, not—"

She silenced Pax with a sudden whip of her hand through the air. "Do you and your brother share everything?"

Pax still wasn't clear where this was going or how it had spun off track, so he kept to short words. "Most of the time."

"Such as."

Connor cleared his voice and pointed toward the kitchen. "We can step out."

Joel didn't move. If anything, he leaned back farther in his chair.

"No, stay." She said it to them but stared at Pax as she walked around the table and stopped right in front of him.

Not exactly how he liked to unload his family history, but Connor knew most and Joel knew some. There weren't any big surprises here. Nothing happy or fun, either.

Pax crossed his arms over his chest. "Our story isn't all that original anyway. Dad died in a car accident, mom lost it, then lost custody of us, and we were forgotten."

"We? You're referring to this brother I haven't seen?"

Pax sensed some female grumbling but let it slide. This kind of story came out better in one telling. No need to draw it out. "Me and Davis. He's older and more responsible and made sure we were okay. I owe him for that. For a lot of things, actually, but mostly for that."

"Yeah, well, not all of us had that sort of sibling protection."

"Meaning?" But Pax knew. From the pieces he gathered from the news and the longer renditions from her father's criminal file, the readily available statistics about Kelsey's life followed a poor-little-rich-girl theme.

Not that the description and personality type fit Kelsey. There was nothing spoiled or entitled about her. Lost at times, yes, but not limited. If anything, she far surpassed what could be expected from her upbringing and all the negatives handed to her. She had become driven, smart, determined and far too tempting for his control to handle.

But even if he hadn't read the file, even if he'd never read one line about her life or known about her mother's death from cancer, he'd know a secret part of her.

There was an unspoken club for survivors of terrible parents, and her father definitely qualified as that. The offspring who stumbled around, trying to find their equilibrium as they made their way in a world that ignored them and struggled to put the past behind them so it wouldn't infect their futures.

In Kelsey, Pax saw a fellow fighter, someone who stepped up because no one was there to lift her. Someone who refused to be a victim. He recognized the symptoms because he shared them.

"My mom died and my dad's replacement wife stepped in almost immediately." The words spilled out of her slowly at first and then picked up to a tumbling pace. Her gaze darted around the room and finally landed back on Pax with eyes bleak and dark with sadness. "I was the part of the deal she *had* to take, and when Sean came along, she quickly figured out that having me around potentially decreased his share of the family fortune. She took care of that by shipping me off to boarding school and limiting my visits home."

"There's a word for women like that." And Pax was tempted to yell it.

"No arguments here." Kelsey's shoulders slumped. "In her mind, I needed to be ignored, forgotten and kept out of town."

Not a surprise but still hard to hear. The way her family treated her, as an afterthought and nuisance, explained a lot about Kelsey's fierce personality. She fought hard because she'd been taught to do so while a kid.

"I'm sorry." The words were so useless, and he knew they meant almost nothing after hearing them from social workers and well-meaning but ineffective professionals his whole life, but the emotion behind them this time was real.

"My relationship with Sean never had a chance. My already strained bond with my demanding father never recovered after he remarried."

"Not a big loss," Joel mumbled.

"I'm not in the will, which is truly a blessing because in the Moore family money equals power in a very destructive way. I'm not mentioned in any interview or during any conversation. And since I refused to testify for him, I'm not even a thought at the holidays. I can't hide behind the lie of seeing family only at Christmas, because I'm not invited."

Connor frowned. "But your stepmother died."

"I prefer to think of her as my father's wife and eliminate any reference to a real relationship between us, and yes. A car accident some said was fueled by alcohol. I don't know, but I don't doubt it. My father asked me not to come to the funeral, so I stayed away."

One more thing they had in common. Lives touched by car accident tragedies. For Pax, the loss changed everything when he lost a parent. For her, the accident highlighted how little she meant to her dad. Both instances sucked.

The driving need to touch Kelsey shocked Pax. He ached for her loss and the young girl who deserved so much better. The audience and timing stopped him.

Plus he had a bigger point to make. Something he wanted her to see and understand even though he doubted her ability to take it in after everything else she'd been through today. "You're here, helping Sean. There's a tie. Maybe a thin one, and something your father and his mother tried to destroy, but it's there."

This time she did roll her eyes. Didn't put much energy behind it, but she did it. "I'm trying not to get killed and hoping he doesn't, either. I'm not convinced that makes me Sister of the Year."

But maybe she wasn't as alone in the world as she wanted to believe, and Pax hoped she would somehow fight her way through all the confusion and pain and see that. "I think you're doing okay."

"I'm amazed with every minute that passes without me throwing up."

That certainly broke the serious mood enveloping the room. "Makes two of us."

"Look, I think we need to call it a night. It's late and even without the injuries this has been a rough one." Connor kept his death grip on the paperwork as he started issuing orders disguised as suggestions. "Kelsey, there's a room on the third floor you can use. It's a crash pad of sorts. Towels and sheets are clean, and no one will bother you up there."

Joel laughed. "You sure about that?"

Connor set down his mug on the table with a sharp whack and shot Pax a back-off look. "She needs sleep."

"Why are you looking at me?" But Pax knew.

Hands in the air, Joel shook his head. "I'm not touching that comment."

The clapping started a second later. Two quick smacks followed by a men-are-so-annoying sigh had everyone looking at Kelsey. "Before this totally disintegrates into juvenile boys locker room talk, I need to ask one question."

"Only one?" The fact she managed to follow everything going on around her and handle being in the middle of so much danger impressed Pax. He couldn't imagine her taking on one more thing.

"Why would my brother steal this information? I know all the possible answers are bad, so I'm not seeking some made-up response that makes him sound patriotic or noble. What I really want is to get a sense of how much trouble he's in here." She made a deflating sound as she blew out a long breath. "Are we talking about selling to foreign countries or other companies? Is this a treason issue? What are the possibilities here?"

Since holding up his weight on the one side became harder by the second, Pax slipped his thigh on the edge of the table. He hoped to ease the pounding of blood down his leg. "These things generally break down into a few possible motives. Political statement, revenge, sex or money."

"There's no evidence of a woman, or man for that matter,

who has Sean's interest." Joel flipped through the pages of the document as he talked. "From his history, Sean doesn't appear to be a political radical. As for revenge, Kingston gave him a lot of responsibility from the start, so I don't see bad workplace blood, but who knows?"

"So, most likely it's money." She glanced around the room. "He's been brought up to believe he's the sole heir to my father's fortune, but with the court case, claims against his company and a freeze on family funds from Sean's mother's side of the family, I don't think there's much left over for Sean."

"Combine that with the fact he hasn't exactly been taught survival skills to make it on his own, and the opportunity for stupidity and criminal behavior rises," Pax said.

But she had the skills. Pax had seen them, admired them and been a bit in awe of them. But none of that meant Sean could find his way out of a room with an open door. The stunt he pulled with the work documents showed that.

"There are people—governments—who would pay a lot of money for certain information." Connor's voice got softer and his rough demeanor lightened. It was as if he, too, feared causing her more pain. "Do you understand what I'm saying?"

She nodded. "Someone gave Sean access to stuff like that?"

"I was about to ask the same question. But I can see he definitely did by looking at the stuff he smuggled out to you." Joel shook his head as he talked, but most of his focus centered on the page he spread out across his end of the table.

"Kingston recently moved deeper into intelligence work." And from what Pax could tell it had been on the edge of trouble ever since.

He doubted the owner and board of directors at Kingston understood the level of concern by the higher-ups at the Department of Defense. Sean played a dangerous game with some big and deadly players.

"The owner, Bryce Kingston, is supposed to be a brilliant innovator, and he's been working on something called the Signal Reconnaissance Program. It's a way to break into the military communications of other militaries," Connor explained.

"And, of course, someone filled you in about all of this top-secret stuff." She said it as a statement instead of a question.

Pax answered anyway. "Someone at the Pentagon who is more than a little concerned about Kingston's internal security tipped us off. Yes."

Before Pax could launch into a detailed explanation, Connor talked right over him. "Point is, with this program from Kingston the U.S. can monitor not only the movements of foreign military assets but listen in as if they're sitting in the middle of a Russian sub. It's in the testing and development stage, but it's—"

Joel snapped his fingers without lifting his head. "A game changer."

"It will be if it turns out to be effective. The government handed Kingston a lot of R&D money to get this program off the ground. There is a big push to move it into beta testing. Word is the initial trials are positive," Pax said.

She nibbled on her bottom lip as wariness fell over her features. "If Sean got his hands on that program, or parts of it, and knew how it worked...then what?"

Joel finally looked up. "He could make a lot of money. Like, buy-an-island-and-hide-out type of money."

But Pax knew that wasn't the real issue or the one that should matter to Kelsey. He cut right to it. "Or he could end up dead."

Chapter Eleven

Sean walked down the long driveway and crept up to the gate. Trees lined the property, covering all but the smallest peak of the three-story stone house sitting back off the road. He'd grown up in the Virginia mansion, complete with gardeners and maids and a full-time staff. They'd belonged to country clubs, even a ski resort. His life once revolved around parties and private schools and a second home on the beach in Delaware.

That was before. Before the allegations. Before his parents' violent outbursts and vicious fights. Before the police came and the money dried up. Before his mother threatened to walk out but died before she could get the house packed.

Before Kelsey refused to come back and help.

Things were supposed to be different now. Sean made it through the boredom of school and earned some recognition through the math department. He'd turned his love of video games into a real-life application by combining it with his natural ability at calculations.

He had a job and a life, or he did until a few weeks ago when it all turned upside down. He'd been tasked with a top-secret project and subjected to random drug tests and other unnecessary security measures.

The lie detector was the worse. Strapped to a chair and a machine and forced to answer moronic questions. It was all a waste of his time. He wanted to work, not get bogged down in stupid crap.

One day he signed in, fine-tuned the program, fixed the mistake and left without leaving a data footprint. Just as he was supposed to do. He'd been promised easy and unseen. Sneak the files out and act as if nothing happened.

He did everything he was told and didn't tip off any alarms. But then men started following him and his studio apartment got turned upside down. The few possessions he owned and had taken with him that weren't frozen in his father's mess had been broken and destroyed.

He'd been on the run ever since. With a limited cash flow and few places to go, he'd ended up here. Amazing that no matter how hard he tried to break free, he ended up back here.

Bryce Kingston knew the truth and now someone wanted Sean dead, so even this house might not protect him.

He threw his bag over the top of the fence as he'd done hundreds of times as a kid. Back then beating the security system had been a game. Now it was a necessity. Using the metal rails of the gate, he grabbed on to the decorative knobs and wedged his sneakers in between the bars.

He'd spent most of the past few years sitting at a computer, but he wasn't out of shape. With a grunt and a concentrated yank, he climbed. Swinging his leg over the top, he skipped the rest of the vault and jumped down.

The night's hot air blew around him as he fell, but he misjudged the distance and dropped longer than expected. He hit the soft grass with a sickening thud. His feet hit and one ankle overturned.

One minute he stood and the next his leg buckled, dragging him down. He dropped as he called out. Rolling around on the ground, holding his leg and swearing into the dark night, he tried to work out the kink.

He froze when lights clicked on over his head. A whirring

sound echoed around him. One he couldn't place. He'd just struggled to a sitting position when footsteps thudded by his head and something hard nailed him in the back. His face smashed into the turf and grass filled his mouth. Shifting and struggling, he pushed up and turned to the side, breathing in a huge gulp of air despite the weight pounding against him.

He braced to flip over when he heard a distinct click. He'd never heard the exact sound before, but combined with the hard metal pushing against the back of his skull it wasn't a mystery. After all that running he'd been found.

"Do not move."

At the sound of the stern voice, Sean let out a loud exhale. His shoulders slumped in relief. "Hello, Dad."

Fingers dug into Sean's arm and then turned him over. His father loomed above, hands on his hips and wearing a golf shirt and khakis, the daily uniform he'd adopted after prison.

Gone were the expensive suits and shiny watches. He insisted those days were behind him, along with his ability to earn a "decent" living. Resting on the money still in his bank while his attorneys went unpaid qualified as roughing it to Dad.

Sanford Moore, Sandy to friends, as well as to those who believed he'd defrauded them and the journalists on the talk show circuit who enjoyed bringing him on their programs even now, stared down with fury turning his face purple. "What are you doing sneaking onto my property?"

Sean wasn't sure when he'd become a visitor in his family home. "I needed somewhere to hide."

"You come through the front door or you don't bother coming home at all. And you call first. You're a grown-up now. Act like it."

Since the family's finances no longer allowed for paid guards and a top-of-the-line security system, Sean thought

going in quietly was the answer. Just in case someone followed him here. "I didn't want to put you in danger."

"Why do you think I have the gun?"

"I have no idea. When did you get that?" Sean couldn't
believe anyone would sell him one.

"I still have people dropping by the gate, whining about
losing money and blaming me."

Sean had heard the complaint every day for nine years and
didn't have the time to argue about it now. "I know, Dad."

"Then you should know better than to be skulking around
in the dark." His father glanced around. "Where's your car?
I didn't see it drive up."

That answered the question of whether the security cameras still worked. Sean could imagine his father spending
hours a day sitting over them, watching the screens. His paranoia had bloomed into a restless living thing, and with his
professional reputation in tatters, all he had was the money
from Sean's mother's estate—the part her relatives couldn't
figure out how to take—plus the money for the book he'd
just sold. The same money every fraud victim wanted to grab
away before his father could spend it.

"I don't have my car. I hitched." Three drivers and a drop-
off a mile away, but Sean got there.

The clenched jaw suggested his father was not impressed.
"Have you lost your mind?"

Sean was starting to wonder. "Someone's following me."

"Because of me." His father reached down and jerked
Sean to his feet. The gun stayed within sight but was no
longer aimed.

Sean suspected that could change at any moment. His father's temper was well-known, and Sean tried very hard not
to tweak it. "No, because of *my* work."

The older man's eyes narrowed right before he turned and

faced the house. He took three steps before looking over his shoulder and motioning Sean to join him. "What did you do?"

Despite the throbbing ankle, Sean grabbed his bag and rushed to keep up. "Nothing."

"Come on, Sean."

He brushed the overgrown branches out of the way, making a path through a group of trees that were once manicured to perfection weekly by a small staff. "I have some work documents and now I'm in some trouble."

His father eyed him. "What kind of documents?"

No way was Sean divulging every last piece of information. Kelsey had called him naive when he'd stuck up for their father years ago. She never understood that he saw Dad's flaws.

Sean could also look at the numbers and see how, if the market hadn't taken a sudden downturn, Dad could have replaced the missing money and made a fortune for his clients. It was a money game, and for years he'd landed on the winning side, until the one time he didn't and everything fell apart.

But Sean also learned from Kelsey's mistakes. She took Dad on directly. Sean preferred to play the role of loyal son and pick his battles. This wasn't one. "Important documents about government programs."

"You have these documents on you?"

His dad's visual tour suggested he was a second or two away from hunting for them in Sean's jeans and baggy shirt. "I mailed them to Kelsey."

His dad stopped then. Fury washed over his features, pushing his mouth down and pulling the skin tight over his cheeks. "What were you thinking? She's not an ally. Ever. Kelsey is out for one person and one person only—Kelsey."

Sean knew the look and recognized the building rage, and

he didn't welcome either. "I figured no one would look for me near her. It's not a secret we're estranged."

His father scoffed. "*Estranged.* Ridiculous word."

"No one would suspect I'd confide in her, and she isn't interested in anything about my life. She'll dump the package in her house and forget it."

"She could get rid of it."

Sean doubted that. Not a box. She might open it and ignore it. He couldn't see her throwing it away. After all, she'd kept the handwritten notes Father told her to throw away all those years ago. The same ones that outlined Father's deposits into accounts he claimed not to own. Instead of listening, she'd kept everything and turned it all over to the prosecution.

Their father would never forgive her for that betrayal, but it suggested to Sean he'd picked the right person to hold the documents. "She has a history of holding on to things. Important things."

They stood in silence. Neither moved as the motion sensor light over their heads flickered to life. Finally, his father nodded. "True."

"But now I need the papers and calculations. The few times I've been able to borrow a phone I haven't been able to reach her."

His father swore and then started walking again, his long legs and large frame eating up the distance to the house in minutes. "Figures."

"I thought I could try to reach her from here."

"Kelsey does owe me." A smile kicked across his father's face. "Maybe it's time Kelsey comes home and does her duty."

KELSEY CHANGED INTO the pajama shorts set Connor found for her in his wife's things and dropped back on the mattress. The soft comforter swallowed Kelsey, and a pile of pillows propped her head up. She stared at the ceiling with the intricate moldings and fancy light dropped on a chain right above the double bed and tried to imagine Pax moving around on the floor above. The footsteps had faded, so she strained to get a sense of him. No luck so far.

She expected a makeshift cot on a cramped third floor. They'd described the third floor as a crash pad, and that just did not sound appealing to her at all, but she'd sleep curled up on the floor if it meant a few hours for her to rest.

The day had been long and exhausting. Every time she closed her eyes she saw bodies piled up around her. Keeping them open didn't exactly blink the visual image totally away either, but the memory lessened.

After some grumbling and arguing between Pax and Connor, she'd been assigned to the guest room on the second floor, the same floor she now knew acted as Connor's home. And Pax wandered silently somewhere above in the so-called crash pad and managed to be quiet about it.

Because of the high mattress, her feet barely grazed the floor. She swung the one, letting her bare foot ease across the fluffy carpet. From the canopy bed to the soft blue walls, the room telegraphed comfort. It could be in a magazine, the kind she paged through and drooled over. She guessed Connor's wife deserved the credit.

But it wasn't her apartment, and Kelsey couldn't get around that. Humble and made up of mismatched second-hand furniture, that apartment belonged solely to her. Her hard work shaped it. Not being there, not being able to protect it or serve her customers daily as she'd done since she'd taken over the place made her antsy.

Her skin jumped and shifted, pulling to get free, just thinking about the ruined inventory and lost profits. The mortgage company wouldn't care that her inability to pay was somehow her brother's fault. She barely understood the connections reaching from his actions to her livelihood. She doubted anyone else would, either.

She turned her head and glanced out the window. The panes looked normal, but she guessed there was some sort of voodoo security film coating on them. Still, they were shut. The cool breeze in the room came from the air conditioner vent blowing across her body. Everything she needed to sleep was there—cool room, comfortable bed and complete safety.

Everything but Pax.

A soft tap on the door dragged her attention away from the dark sky outside. She glanced over in time to see Pax walk into the room. *Limp in* was more accurate. He wore navy sweats and a tee and he'd never looked better to her. Broad shoulders, muscled arms and a face that made her sigh a little inside when he glanced in her direction even for a second.

She sat up, balancing her upper body on her elbows. A smile inched across her face before she could catch it. On some level she'd known he would come. The house grew quiet and everyone talked about rest, but she knew in her soul he would wait and then visit. She guessed that's why he fought against her being placed right across the hall from Connor's bedroom—no privacy.

He leaned back against the door without venturing farther into the private space. "You okay?"

"I should be comatose with sleep by now."

"Sometimes it's hard to shake off the adrenaline rush and calm down. And heaven knows you've been through a lot today. Men coming at you, me shoving you around."

Funny how she'd long forgiven him. All that anger drained away until her focus shifted to wanting him around. "I got used to the last part."

"Oh, yeah?" His eyebrows lifted.

"Yeah."

He pushed off the door and came deeper into the room.

Instead of stopping a respectable distance away and keeping up the charade of bodyguard/client, he sat down on the bed next to her.

The move had her sitting the whole way up and leaning in close. She blamed his greater weight and the way the mattress dipped around him, but deep inside she knew the truth. She was right where she wanted to be...with him.

She ran a palm over his knee and waited for any sign of pain. If he even flinched, she'd wake Joel. "How's the leg?"

"Medicated to the point of being numb."

That explained the glassy look to Pax's eyes. "Did you really get shot?"

"I can show you the wound." He messed up his naughty innuendo and wiggling eyebrows by picking up her hand and holding it in his. So soft and gentle. So opposite of the guy who fired guns and threw knives. "The bullet was coming and it was either me or Lara, Davis's new wife. I picked me."

Between the words and the touch, Kelsey's heart flipped. "Sounds heroic."

"Not really."

She'd bet Lara would disagree. And if it turned out that Lara was one of those entitled types who didn't praise Pax for his bravery, Kelsey might just punch her. "Will the wound always hurt?"

He leaned in, meeting her part way, until their shoulders touched. "I get a lot of 'we'll have to see' type of responses from doctors and physical therapists. I feel as if I've been off it and taking it easy forever. I'm ready to be back to normal again."

From the serious expression and continued brushing of his thumb over the back of her hand, she guessed he actually believed what he'd just said. "You think today qualified as being off your leg?"

"Sure."

Men never ceased to fascinate her. Even the good ones said odd things, and she knew for certain from everything she'd seen and experienced that he fell into that category. "Interesting."

"Either way, it seems clear I won't get full use back."

She tried to imagine what being limited in any physical way did to a man like him. He rescued and saved. Not being able to do that could break him. Could endanger the work he appeared to love. "Does that bother you?"

"Bother?"

The repeated question sounded like a stall to her. "You're familiar with the word, right? *Upset you, anger you, tick you off.* Any of those, or do you shrug and take it all in stride?"

He lifted their joined hands and kissed the back of hers. "All injuries are bad, but the only ones you need to worry about are the ones you don't survive."

"Wow, that's…"

His mouth lifted in a half smile. "True?"

"Maudlin."

He threw back his head and laughed, deep and throaty, genuine and free. "Says the woman who's been mauled and attacked and shot at today."

The laugh still rumbled through her even after he stopped talking. She tried to think of one thing about him that turned her off and couldn't come up with anything. From his looks to the emotional depth hinted at behind those eyes and in his words, she got sucked in.

After all those months of keeping her life commitment free. All those other guys who stuck around but meant nothing. She finally found someone who challenged and excited her. She just wished the danger he walked into so willingly didn't scare her so much.

But that didn't mean they couldn't have a moment.

She rested her cheek against his shoulder and inhaled the scent of soap on his skin. "Have I thanked you?"

He shrugged. "That's not necessary."

She knew he'd say that. Her head dropped, inching closer to his collarbone and that delicious spot, the dip where bones met muscle at the base of his neck. "Oh, Pax, ignoring my compliments makes it very hard to seduce you."

He leaned back and looked down at her, the smile softer but possibly deeper, and those eyes darkened and so appealing. "Is that what's happening?"

She wanted to say yes. She could have said yes and been telling the truth. The bed, the room, the heat bounced between them. It didn't take a genius to figure out where they were headed.

"Not quite, but I am trying to get you to kiss me as you promised earlier." She lifted her head as she said it, making sure to drop her lips right below his.

"You could just ask."

His whispered words blew across her lips. "I was kind of hoping I didn't have to.

"So we're clear—" he rubbed his thumb along her bottom lip "—I want to almost every second of the day. I see you and my brain misfires. To protect you I should step back, maybe let Joel take over, but the idea of someone else being with you, touching you, is more than I can tolerate."

Her hand played with the scruff on the tip of his chin. "I wouldn't let anyone else touch me."

"What about me?"

"You can touch me as much as you want." She whispered the response because it felt right to let the words dance softly off her tongue.

After that his mouth dipped and his lips slipped over hers. Heat beat off her body and blood rushed to her head. Sensations walloped her—dizziness, elation. She craved his touch and wrapped her arms around his neck to pull him in closer.

The light touch of a firm mouth morphed into a blinding kiss. The gentle brush of lips against lips gave way to a devouring need. His mouth slanted and his hands roamed. Palms pressed against her back as his lips traveled over hers.

His body surrounded her, slipped over hers. Air rushed out of her and she couldn't draw enough in, but she didn't care.

Before she knew what was happening, her back hit the mattress and his firm body hovered over hers. The kiss set off explosions throughout her body. Her skin heated and her nails dug into his shirt.

One hand speared through his hair as his mouth pressed against hers and their tongues met. She recognized the pounding she heard as a kick up in their breathing. If her heart hammered any harder, she'd need an ambulance.

The kiss went on forever but didn't last nearly long enough. When he lifted his head for air, she balked and found his mouth again. His palm spread over her bare stomach, and her fingers inched under the band of his tee.

She was ten seconds away from begging him to strip off her shirt when a door banged in the hallway.

They both jumped. Pax jackknifed to a sitting position and she bounced on the bed, shifting just outside of his grip. The sudden separation left her skin cold and her mind reeling. She could actually feel her head spin as the wonderful, sexy tension dissipated.

"What was that?" She nearly panted out the words.

The bed creaked as Pax shifted his weight. "If I had to guess, I'd say Connor."

The anger in Pax's voice had her blinking even as she tried to understand the sentence. "What?"

"I think he's warning me to use my head."

Sitting next to him, she slipped a hand over Pax's back,

loving the ripple of his muscles underneath, and then wrapped the other arm around his stomach. "He cares if we're together?"

Pax's hand brushed up and down her bare arm. "Only if it means we're not safe."

"Am I safe with you?"

He faced her then, all traces of fury gone. "Always."

"Well, then—"

"And to prove it I'm going to be a gentleman and leave." He finished the vow with a quick kiss on her mouth.

She wanted more but he'd pulled back and away. Not at all what she wanted. "We seem to be experiencing a communication issue."

He opened his mouth and closed it twice before finally getting a word out. "Not at all, but you need rest."

She was all for the chivalry thing, but this might be too much. "Really?"

"But tomorrow…"

The promise hung right there. She could see it in the soft shine of his eyes and quirk of his mouth. "Yes?"

With one final kiss—this one lingered longer and held a touch of teasing—he stood up. "Get some sleep and you'll find out."

Chapter Twelve

Pax came downstairs just after six the next morning. The sun already beamed in the window by the front door, casting shadows across the hardwood entry floor. He took a sharp turn at the bottom of the stairs and went through the sliding doors into what he always thought of as the War Room. The news played on one of the television screens and a police scanner buzzed in the background.

Joel already sat at the bank of computers, tapping on a keyboard and scanning the screens in front of him as he typed. A pile of papers from Sean's box sat next to his left hand and more were scattered at his feet.

Between his messed-up hair and rumpled clothing, Pax wondered if Joel bothered to sleep last night. It was quite possible he hadn't moved from that chair since Pax left him six hours ago.

Connor was a different story. Dress shirt and pants— check. Hair combed and watch in place—check. If the man slept Pax didn't think it was for very long. He bounced up every morning looking as if he could walk into an important meeting at the Pentagon. And sometimes he did just that.

Munching on toast and downing a cup of coffee, Connor walked around the table and grabbed the newspaper off the edge of Joel's workstation. From the pot, it looked as if he carried his second or third cup.

Caffeine fueled the man, and since he had Corcoran running with little trouble and just the right amount of oversight, Pax didn't argue with the method.

"You crash here?" he asked Joel.

"I used the couch. Made more sense than running back and forth to my place." Joel glanced away from the screen for more than his usual second. "Where did you sleep, or am I too young and impressionable to know?"

"Feel free to shut up."

"Hey, if it's easier for me to make it up in my head, say the word and I'll start."

Sometimes the limited sleep and a prolonged lack of female influence had the conversation dipping into the junior-high level. Pax was grateful Kelsey stayed upstairs and missed this part. "Third floor. I was up there alone."

Connor snorted. "Not for lack of trying."

Which brought up another complaint. "Subtle and well-timed door slam, by the way. You'll be great if you ever have teen girls."

"It's my house." Connor didn't lift his head but he smiled.

"Any reason for the angry-father routine other than the obvious explanation that you're watching over me?"

"You're a big boy and your love life only matters to the extent it creeps into the office."

A slow anger snuck up on Pax out of nowhere. "Which never happens."

"Until now," Joel mumbled without turning around.

"For the record, I'm not watching you. I'm watching over Kelsey." Connor blew on his coffee and then gulped half of it down. "Is she still sleeping?"

Thinking about her in bed, the mattress and those little shorts…yeah, that was the last place Pax wanted his mind wandering unchecked this morning. Not at work. Not now. Certainly not in front of his friends.

He reached for a clean mug on the tray in the middle of the table. "I want her to get as much rest as possible. Yesterday was a fairly rotten day for us, and we're trained. Supposedly we are accustomed to this stuff, but she isn't. She's a civilian and I don't want to lose sight of that because she happens to have a fighter streak that rivals ours."

Connor dropped the newspaper on the table and poured Pax a mug before refilling his own. "Point taken."

"You conceded that argument kind of fast." Which Pax knew from experience meant bad news would slam into him any second.

"It's early." Connor made the dry statement before taking his seat at the head of the table.

That put Joel and Connor at one end and Pax on the other. Something about the setup reminded him of being called to the principal's office as a kid. Back then pulling a fire alarm struck him as a challenge. Thank goodness he'd gotten smarter as he aged or he'd likely be in a prison cell.

"Since you're down here instead of upstairs where it's more interesting and clearly need to find something to do to keep your mind off the woman upstairs—" Connor turned the pages of the paper with an annoying slowness "—you may as well know we have a new problem."

And here we go.

Joel spun his chair around to sit next to Connor and face Pax head-on. "A big problem."

"You really need to stop saying stuff like that." Pax looked at the plate of doughnuts and muffins in front of him, wanting to ignore Joel's newest issue.

"Sorry, but it's unavoidable," Joel said, sounding the exact opposite of sorry.

The crinkling sound of the paper as Connor refolded it ripped through Pax's brain. If they wanted his attention, they had it. He dropped the doughnut and stood with his hands at his back and legs apart, braced for whatever was about to come.

"Tell Pax before the nosiness kills him." Connor put his hand over the top of the oversized mug Jana bought him one year as a joke and which he'd used ever since. A file slid down the table with a whoosh and landed exactly in front of Pax. Joel nodded, satisfaction obvious on his face that he managed to spin the papers that far and complete the landing. "Someone tapped your personnel file."

Pax's hand stopped halfway to the file. "What?"

"You're been investigated, or at the very least checked out." Joel put a second file in front of Connor, who didn't even open it.

For someone in Pax's position, the news spelled disaster. He no longer worked in black ops under false names, with limited contacts and constant moving around. Those days had ended when he'd left government service and thrown in with Connor.

But his current position required a certain level of confidentiality. People couldn't know background information on him or where he lived, which at the moment, with his boat gone, amounted to right upstairs in the crash pad.

That's why having his boat ownership uncovered in his last active job proved such a mess. A mole related to the NCIS case had uncovered the title information, tracked him down and almost blown up Davis and Lara in the process. Finding out someone new had started excavating and bumped into his file ticked Pax off.

"How exactly did that happen? This stuff is supposed to be sealed." Pax scowled at Joel. "By you."

"I'm the temporary tech guy, but I see your point."

"It's bad for all of us, Pax. Not just you." Connor opened the cover of the file and then closed it again without reading a word. "We all have confidential files. Even if someone broke into the DOD database and found your name, that's all the information the person could get."

Pax used to buy that. He knew Connor still did, but Pax had reason to be skeptical. "I have a thousand pieces of a blown-up boat and a bullet in my thigh that suggest otherwise."

The release of all private information, any information, required a top-secret clearance. Even then, the person checking had to be read into the specific program and have a need to know. Not just anyone could go tripping through. Their files were purposely hard to locate, and anyone who did wasn't just stumbling around for fun. But that didn't mean Pax trusted everything to work as planned.

Joel stuttered a bit while glancing back and forth between Pax and Connor, but he got the words out. "Tracing the breach back to its source, someone did a facial recognition search on you and landed on your government file. That means the person had access to high-level recognition software."

Connor shook his head as if he were reasoning it all out. "We're talking about someone with clearance and skills. Someone who could get in and out without raising a flag."

Before Pax could ask a million questions about his identity being compromised and what that would mean for the caseload, Joel spoke again, this time much louder until his voice carried over them all. "Before you both panic, though I think I'm a second too late, the person looking only got as far as your sealed file. The security held. Everything worked as it was supposed to."

The knot in Pax's gut didn't untie. "You're sure?"

"There was nothing to see, but DOD has a program that flashes us a warning whenever anyone comes checking up on us. Without that we wouldn't even know. It's an extra layer meant to make us feel more confident, not cause unnecessary panic."

No one had ever accused Pax of panic before. Before the anger could fester and explode, Pax tramped it back down again. He was willing to chalk the entire conversation up to Joel's lack of sleep and Pax's stupid injury that refused to heal.

The leg made the others wary. He understood the concern, but he wasn't the type to get injured and then hide in the house, and it was time for all of them to deal with that fact. "The worry feels necessary to me since it was my file."

Connor held out a hand to stop whatever had Joel leaning forward. "I think what Joel means is, we now have a warning system, though it is true we also have a problem because someone *was* checking on you and we can't ignore that."

When the bad news came, it sure seemed to come in waves. Just once Pax wanted an easy case with a simple answer. This wasn't it. He tried to imagine when "this" had happened. Never that he could recall.

"Okay, so someone tripped this warning program, right?" Pax despised this part of the job. The constant scrutiny. The checking and rechecking. The reality that he forfeited privacy when he decided to serve his country.

"Yes." Joel reached behind him and dragged his wireless keyboard onto the conference table in front of him.

It wasn't like Joel to give a quick answer, not when it came to this stuff. The sudden lack of eye contact raised a red flag for Pax. "Can we trace it back to the actual person behind the facial recognition check?"

"Not quite that far." Joel tapped on the keys as lines of code scrolled across one of the screens behind him. "The guy has cover and knows how to go undetected."

"But you did find him. You detected him."

Joel glanced up with a smile. "Because I'm better and I

will trace the file breach back to someone, though I think we all have an idea where this started."

Connor nodded. "Exactly. Ground zero is the coffee shop. You were there every day but you happened to be out on the street in front of it with Kelsey right before the file breach occurred."

With that Pax's next breath wheezed out of his lungs. "You're not saying that she—"

"He's saying the person following her spied you out in the open, likely on the sidewalk, and decided to investigate." Connor didn't say "don't be ridiculous," but the vibe was there under his words.

"By now they've seen the confidential warning on the file. It's not subtle. See for yourself." A few more taps and the monitor on the top right of the panel blinked to life.

Joel and Connor spun around to look at the screen. Pax's face, or a slightly younger version, with a black bar stamped Confidential across it filled the screen. "If the person looking has any sense or experience, he'll know he stumbled onto something big."

"DOD was notified when we were," Connor said.

"Since when?" Pax wasn't clear on when they'd added all these levels of security, but he was grateful for whatever redundancies and fail-safes were in place.

Joel raised his hand. "That was the deal. I wanted the warning as a precaution. DOD only agreed to the install after I gave them the program to use with their other files. They also threw around allegations of 'hacking' but I ignored that."

"You forgot to mention that part to me," Connor said.

Joel shrugged. "Point is our contact should be calling Connor within the next fifteen minutes to report all of this. Connor here gets to act surprised."

"Why does everyone look as if their favorite puppy died?" Kelsey asked the question from the doorway to the main entry. She wore the same pajama shorts but hid most of them under an oversized sweatshirt pulled over the tiny sleep top.

Pax had to fight the urge to carry her upstairs and finish the kissing they'd started last night. "Apparently someone has a photo of me and is doing a search through my work file."

She let her head fall back against the wood. "And you think this is related to Sean?"

"Don't you?"

She huffed and shook her head. Did the whole men-are-so-clueless repertoire as she walked into the room and stopped next to Pax's chair. "Not to state the obvious, but you have other cases. I'm guessing you have enemies."

He held a hand to his heart and pretended to be offended. "I'm wounded that you would think that."

"Gee, what was I thinking?"

"You have to admit, Kelsey, the timing is suspicious." Connor motioned toward the coffeepot and started pouring when she nodded. "But to be sure, Joel will do a deeper trace and we'll double-check."

She took the mug and grasped it in a double-fisted clench. "But right now the evidence points toward Sean and this case."

"Kingston is someone with the skills and resources to break into law enforcement systems and run illegal checks." Joel sat back in his chair. "In fact, it's possible they let him use the programs. He designs the things and is in the intelligence business now. In theory he's not a threat. His risk level should be low."

"Theory." That one word shifted everything in Pax's head. So much for hanging around and letting her reboot.

The Corcoran Team had rules and protocols for this sort of breech. Having Kelsey at his side didn't change any of his core responsibilities. The precautions were there for all of their safety. In this case, Kelsey's safety was paramount, and that meant a change.

"Did you have more to add, or are you only repeating after Joel for some reason?" she asked.

Pax held up a finger. "The risk is low in theory. We don't know the reality."

She sighed as she dropped into the seat next to him. "And why do I think that comment means something bad for me?"

Not the word he would use. *"Bad?"*

"Annoying, then."

Pax couldn't help but smile. "Smart woman."

Chapter Thirteen

They stayed at the Corcoran Team headquarters all day, poring over the contents of the box from Sean and deciphering what the men in the room referred to as code. Kelsey thought the lines resembled gibberish. While the guys pored and deciphered, she read up on the Kingston corporation and its off-the-radar but very wealthy owner.

She asked about a billion questions about the team's past cases, only about three of which they agreed to answer. Really, that was three more than she expected. The questions mostly kept her mind off her store and the inventory rotting on the counters.

And that kiss. She dreamed about that one.

The ongoing discussions also gave her a front-row seat to their logic and problem solving. Their gun skills bordered on amazing, but their intelligence was much more impressive. In the case of Pax, it was off-the-charts attractive.

And by sitting there she could close her eyes and enjoy the men's voices and smile over their verbal jabs at each other. Something about being around the three of them soothed her. The ever-elusive Ben even called in and she met him via teleconference. He had a face and everything.

Not that she cared about any face except Pax's. Watching him work, seeing him concentrate while his expression turned serious and he poured all of his formidable focus into a project...downright sexy. At one point she'd whispered his name just to have all of that attention shift to her. His eyes, cloudy at first, cleared and a smile tugged at the corner of his mouth.

Doubly sexy.

No question that despite a flip-flopping stomach and concerns about her impending poverty, the day went well. No one tried to kill her or shoot at her. She didn't fall down the stairs. Amazing how twelve hours of straight terror could alter what you viewed as a good day. Her bar was low enough that surviving warranted a cake and coffee celebration.

But that was the afternoon. This was now.

The dark and humid night had taken a turn that started an unwelcome shiver rocketing through her. They walked on the creaky dock at a marina about a half mile from the City Dock. Metal clanged on metal as the boats' sails whipped around in the warm prestorm breeze.

With each step, water sloshed and churned. The path below her seemed to bobble and sway as they walked down the lines of slips, almost every one filled with a boat bearing a whimsical name, such as *Lady Luck* or *My Children's Inheritance*.

She'd clearly forgotten to mention the whole terror-at-the-thought-of-water thing to Pax. She lived in a water resort town and vowed never to go on another boat. She stayed away from the ocean, the nearby Chesapeake and large pools. Well, she did until Pax dragged her here tonight.

He moved along, his long legs eating up the dock several planks at a time and showing only the slightest limp. She doubted anyone who didn't know could pick up on the injury.

Every now and then his foot fell too hard and his weight shifted ever so slightly. She knew because she stared him down with practiced tunnel vision. It was either that or give in to the violent tremors rolling through her.

Her breath raced up her throat and got caught there. She swallowed it back. "One question."

"Hit me."

She slid her hand in his and felt her heart hiccup when his fingers tightened around hers. "What are we doing here?"

"Protocol says—"

"If one of you is under scrutiny then you separate from the team headquarters to assess the danger. The team is never exposed." Those words had been drummed into her brain. "Yeah, I got that part this afternoon. Connor isn't exactly subtle when he launches into the live version of your office manual. That guy can talk."

Pax's warm laughter filled the quiet night. "The type of training he provides and the relentless repetition make us good at what we do. Without it, we'd likely be shot at even more often."

"There's a scary thought."

"His lectures can be annoying, but they are effective if for no other reason than you only want to hear them once."

"I won't even ask where Connor learned all those undercover skills, since you'd never tell me anyway." Her nerves kept zapping but the frequency lessened when she heard the mumble of conversation and a stray booming laugh in the distance.

She peeked through the bobbing boats and over the rows to a double-decker boat with lights that outlined its deck. People moved around and hung near the sides. She couldn't make out faces or even the sex of some from this distance, but she knew fun, and that crowd sounded like fun.

"Good call on the too-much-information-about-Connor issue. He's not an oversharer in general and even less so when it comes to his work past. It's part of what makes him good at his job," Pax said.

"I figured it was a need-to-know thing like everything

else about you guys." The calmer mood broke into a wild-frenzy panic inside her when she heard a splash. She jerked back and scanned the water.

"What's wrong?"

A completely irrational fear of big fish. "Nothing."

"Really?"

Something slipped up and out of the waves and then disappeared again. She kept an eye on the spot, waiting for a repeat performance. "Back to my original question. What are we doing at the marina?"

"We need to stay overnight somewhere until the facial recognition thing works itself out." He guided them to the right and steered them past an older couple walking back toward the shore.

She wanted to follow those two to dry land. To anywhere that wasn't here.

"I thought we were going to a hotel." She strained to remember the conversation.

All that talk about an alternate location. Pax had her pack a few things, most of them belonging to Connor's wife. Even now Pax carried the bag over his outside shoulder.

"We're staying on a boat. Not mine because it's gone. It wasn't moored here anyway. It was at another marina, but that cover is blown."

No matter how many words he said, her reaction was the same—*no way.*

She stopped under a light and nearly had her arm ripped off when it took him a few more steps to realize he walked alone.

He turned around, one hand already on the gun she knew he carried. He scanned the area and the smile downshifted into a serious scowl. "What's going on?"

A horn sounded in the distance. The droning matched the heaviness tugging at her. "We have a problem."

The bag fell off his shoulder and hit the deck. His gaze landed everywhere but on her as his gun swept across the landscape. "What did you see?"

The water rippled and the creature made a second appearance. It stayed up for a few beats and then slid under again. The sight had icy fingers clawing at her insides. "First, what was that?"

He lowered the gun. "Wait, what are you…did you see someone or not?"

"I'm serious. Right there." She pointed at the spot where the malformed head stuck up a second ago. It would come up again. It had to or Pax would think she lost her mind.

"It's water, Kelsey. The night makes it look more ominous, but it's nothing but the wind kicking up."

"I'm talking about the big mound that keeps popping up." She ventured a few inches closer to the side of the dock but shifted her weight to her back leg to keep from falling in. "I'm thinking monster fish, shark or a distant relative of the Loch Ness Monster."

He slid his gun back into the holster under his arm. "Okay, fill me in on what's really going on here."

As if she was going to tell some big hero dude about her small fears. Talking made it sound so much sillier, so she forced down the anxiety screaming through her and tried to step around him. "Just asking a question. Let's keep walking."

He caught her arm. "Uh, Kelsey?"

She tried to tug her arm loose but Pax held on. He didn't move, either. If the raised eyebrow was any indication, he didn't intend to.

Fine. Humiliation it would be. "The water makes me crazy."

"Crazy?"

"Like makes me want to crawl out of my skin."

"Okay." The light above them cast strange shadows around them but the stunned look on his face was very visible. "Are we talking water in general or—"

"The salty, dead-fish smell. The constant movement. The fear of drowning. Add it all together and it's taking all of my control not to double over."

"Okay."

"I think it's the wide-open space and lack of control I'd have in there, but I'm not a hundred percent sure. I haven't taken the time to explore the fear in depth. Avoiding it is easier." This wasn't the first time she'd threatened to lose a meal, but this time he handled it better. Seemed to ignore the possibility completely.

Little did he know the real threat was her bursting into tears. Unless Pax had some male gene the rest of his species missed, the weeping thing could be the one issue to bring him to his knees.

"You're really afraid of water?" he asked.

The word was so small for such a big source of paralyzing panic. But she refused to be embarrassed about this. Maybe if she carried a gun and could shoot the sharks, it would be a different story.

"I am, which makes me a very smart woman. The ocean is huge, and humans are tiny by comparison. You do the math."

"Sorry I didn't ask first." He wiped a hand through his hair. "Honestly, I didn't even think about it."

"Because you're not afraid of anything."

He blew out a breath and then picked up the bag and slung it over his shoulder again. "Wrong."

Right.

"Name one thing." She inched away from the edge and closer to him. If she fell in, she wanted him with her. That way she had a shot at going out of this world with one last kiss.

"Lara gets motion sickness, so I know boats aren't for everyone. I just assumed with the way you were raised..." He screwed up his lips and made a face. "Guess not."

Kelsey got caught on the Lara reference and the rest of the comment zinged by before she could process it. Time to back up. "Care to finish that sentence you left there in the middle?"

"Your father used to sponsor a boat racing team. He owned sailboats."

For a few seconds at a time she could forget they didn't have a normal relationship, that Pax didn't know every last detail about her messed-up past. But he did.

Still, there were some things that likely didn't make it into a list of facts in some government file. "My terror was the subject of endless enjoyment to my father."

"I see." Pax's expression stayed blank.

She tried to read him but couldn't. After a quick check of the party boat to make sure the music and laughter went on, she turned back to Pax. "What does that mean?"

"This, the water thing, it all connects to your father." Pax shrugged. "Makes sense."

She refused to let this be some sort of father-induced phobia. "It's about being afraid of dying."

He nodded. "Okay."

For some reason, his automatic-understanding reaction lit a match to her fury. Anger poured over the trembling fear, bringing heat back into her body. "Yeah, I know it's okay."

After a tense minute of rocking boats and clapping water, he pivoted and faced the shore and small store at its edge. He held out a hand to her. "Come on. We'll find another sleeping solution."

Here she was raging and hovering right on the verge of yelling, and he took it. So clear and calm, so utterly accepting of her craziness.

All the indignation rushed right back out of her, leaving her shoulders curling in on her. "That's it?"

His squinting eyes and flat lips could be described only as a look of confusion. "What, did you think I was going to throw you in the murky waves and watch you panic?"

Actually... "You wouldn't be the first one to do so."

He swore under his breath as he stared at his shoes and shifted his feet. "I want to beat almost every member of your family."

Yeah, that wasn't anger she was feeling right now. Light and relieved, drained and excited. "That's strangely sweet."

He gave her an I'll-never-understand-women frown. "I love sailing. I love the water."

He said it so matter-of-factly, as if he was reading it from a card. Not that she was surprised by the admission. He'd mentioned his destroyed boat about a thousand times in thirty-six hours. She knew all about Davis and Lara hiding on it before someone packed it with explosives.

"I picked up on your water fetish."

"But you being comfortable is more important than a boat or the water. I want you to be somewhere you feel safe, and if it's not here we'll go." No fanfare. No big scene. He just said the words and watched her as he spoke.

Her nerves jangled with a certain awareness from the minute they pulled into the marina parking lot. Before the tingling signaled disaster. Now it lit with a spark of life. His words, his support, turned the dread weighing down every step across the dock into something fresh and clear.

"Well, that's just about the most romantic thing I've ever heard." And that was not an exaggeration. It took all her self-control and a good sniff of the dank water to keep her from climbing on top of him.

He shot her a shy smile. "I have skills."

And he kept dragging more and more out to impress her. "You'd give up sailing for me?"

His head bent to the side and one eye closed as his gaze

drilled into her. "That sounds like you plan to stick around after we save Sean and get you back to work."

The words were out and she couldn't call them back. Smart or not, she'd made it clear this wasn't some sort of adrenaline-fueled temporary thing. She planned to see more of him… on dry land. "I'm finding you hard to get rid of. You seem to have staying power."

"You can count on that, sweetheart." His hand slipped through hers again. They'd taken two steps when his body froze. "Hold up."

The last words came out as a whisper and sliced through her with the force of a knife. Her gaze traveled over the scene in front of her. Boats on each side and a long dock to the few buildings sitting there just on the edge of the parking lot on the shore.

The boats moved. The docks moved. A few people in the distance moved to their cars. Nothing else seemed to move.

"What is it?" Not that she really wanted to know.

He shuffled them behind a sleek racing boat and ducked down, taking her with him. "Two men. Black suits."

The idea was so awful she pretended not to notice how close his foot was to the edge of the dock. The tip of his sneaker actually hung over.

No matter where he stood she couldn't take another gun battle. "No."

"Stay calm." He wrapped an arm around her waist and pulled her in tight to his side. "I need you to trust me."

The light swayed above them from the force of the light summer wind. She took that as a bad sign. "I do."

She balanced her palms against the dock to keep from falling forward. The header almost happened anyway when he slipped the bag off his shoulder and lifted it up and onto the front of the boat they were using as a shield. The bow bumped against the front of the slip as the small waves pushed it forward and back again.

Some people probably liked that sort of thing, found it soothing. She was not one of them.

"We are not getting on that boat." Her throat burned from her effort not to scream the words.

"The men are walking down the floating dock on the other side of this one and have been moving in closer. If they keep going, this area is next on the search."

"Maybe they aren't looking for me."

"How many guys wear black suits and hang out at the marina at night? It's too much of a coincidence to ignore."

Fear shook every cell in her body. "I can't do this."

Any of it. Terror froze everything inside her until she could barely breathe.

"I won't let you fall in."

"Pax, I—"

"I promise. I will hold you and keep you safe, but we need to hide and can use the noise from the movement of the boats as cover."

It all sounded so logical. For some people, jumping out of a plane probably sounded sane. Not her.

He shifted his weight, holding on to her and watching the area around them at the same time. "Ready?"

"No." She'd never even agreed to this stupid plan. Then there was the part where her legs refused to move.

None of that stopped Pax. Without a word, he coaxed and guided. His hand rested on her lower back. He didn't push or shove, but he had her stretching her upper body and one foot leaving the ground.

The material of the boat chilled her warm hands. Shaking with teeth rattling, she lifted one leg and then the other. Waves of fear pummeled her, but she kept her gaze forward and down until she could see only the boat and a small sliver of sky above as she shifted and climbed on board.

Then he was there. His body covered hers as she crawled. The rough feel of the bow dug into her knees, but she didn't stop or let her mind wander to his leg injury for even a second.

Maybe it was her imagination, but she heard the footsteps, slow and steady and coming closer. The men talked but the breeze caught the tone and she couldn't make out the words.

She'd gone a few feet and slid down onto the padded seats when he pulled her with him to the floor of the front seating area and flattened his body over hers. The heat from his skin and the brush of the air had her sweating and sticking to the hard fiberglass underneath her cheek.

She closed her eyes, trying to fight off a new wave of terror, but without a focal point the rocking of the boat had her shifting from side to side. Much more of that and she wouldn't have to be in the water to hate it.

"Nothing here." The stranger's deep voice sounded so close, just above her.

She even held her breath to keep from giving away their location. With her palms against the floor and her body spread as low as possible, she tried to make out the conversation. She'd settle for anything to make all of this worthwhile. One piece could be the difference between her running and getting back to her life.

"We need to check in," another voice said.

The sounds came from all around her. The water, the wind, the men. Everything pressed in on her until she had to bite back the scream rushing up her throat.

It felt like hours before the footsteps grew softer and the quiet of the night took over again. She didn't move but Pax shifted. He slid to the side and all of a sudden the weight was gone. Only the smelly air suffocated her now.

"Wait here." Pax whispered the near-soundless command against her ear.

She stayed plastered to the floor but peeked up at him.

Instead of jumping out of the boat or standing up, he slipped up onto the front bench, seemingly boneless in his movements and not hampered by the leg. Their bag sat on the edge of the boat, and he crouched down as he looked over the area toward the shore.

With a small tap against his ear, he started talking. "Now you can listen because I need eyes here. We had company and I need to know how many more are out there."

Kelsey knew the words went back to Joel and Connor, who would somehow handle it all from a distance. She appreciated the backup plan, but it didn't change the facts in front of her. She wanted off the boat, and her skin itched to jump from it.

"Let's go." He motioned for her to stand up.

She didn't hesitate. "There has to be a hotel around here. Preferably one nowhere near the water."

Every muscle in her body shouted for her to sprint off the boat and right back to the car, but she didn't. Seeing the boats shift and bob around them, watching them bang against the slips, would not ease the fear pulsing through her and scrambling whatever was left in her stomach.

Pax felt around the front of his jeans. "My phone."

Oh, no, no, no. "We can get you a new one."

"It can't be found there. I can lock and wipe it wirelessly, but we don't want to take the risk," Joel said into the comm. "If these guys are fishing based on your love for boating, that's one thing. If they get confirmation you were there, they won't give up on your trail until they pick you up again."

She hated it when Joel got all logical.

Before her brain could signal flight, she dropped back to

the floor and he joined her. The light on the dock didn't reach into this area of the boat, which had made it such a good hiding place but also hard to find anything. They had to pat and feel their way around. Her fingers hit against ropes and hard objects she couldn't identify.

"Got it."

The words had barely left Pax's mouth before she jumped to her feet. She had one leg on the edge of the boat and a winding terror in her gut when Joel's voice cut across the comm again. "They're coming back."

Pax stared at her. "What?"

"Directly for your end of the dock," Connor said. "Move."

Pax pushed her toward the back of the boat and deeper into the darkness surrounded by water. The back of her thigh smacked into the chair by the wheel, and the shot of pain had her vision going black. Her legs got tangled up and her footing fumbled, but Pax's strong arms grabbed her before she hit the floor with a thud. He rushed her forward and had her pressed up against the back edge of the boat in a muscle-cramping crouch when the footsteps and talk closed in.

"I saw it back here," the one with the deeper voice said. "Just sitting there."

"You should have said something the first time."

She didn't know what they were talking about, but the conversation seemed to center on their area. Then she remembered the bag and her head dropped back. They were coming right in her direction.

Dizziness crashed in on her from every side. Pax stood bent over in the shadows, hiding behind the windshield with his body covering hers. But if the attackers came on the boat, the impromptu hiding place would not protect them.

As the attackers' voices grew louder, Pax pressed back

even farther. His butt hit against her stomach and threw her off balance.

She made a stumbling step and her calves hit the edge. A cry for help bounced around her head but her body kept going. She fell over, her hands flapping as she tried to grab on to anything that would break her fall before she slapped against the water. The air whipped through her hair and she held her breath, waiting for the horrible dunk.

Just when she thought she'd hit, her body jerked to a stop and her sneakers splashed in the water. Her eyes flew open and Pax's face filled her vision. He looked at her from his position, bent over the side of the boat and holding her around the waist and one thigh. He'd caught her like a net and left her hanging like dead weight off the side.

"I have you." That's it. A soft whisper that backed up his earlier promise.

In the darkness with attackers lurking and dead weight in his arms, he acted as if none of it added up to a big deal. The individual pieces would break most men, never mind the pileup of problems.

He took it in stride and held on with a death grip that had his fingers digging into her side. His jaw clenched and his forearms shook. He even choked up on his hold when the water splashed into her hair.

The potential attackers had arrived at the front of the boat and even now discussed the bag. Kelsey searched her mind to remember if there was anything in the duffel that gave away their identities. Connor had been very specific about that issue, but she'd thought the worry amounted to overkill. And it would have if they'd actually ended up at a hotel as she expected instead of hanging over the terrifying black water she had avoided for her entire grown-up life.

Her head fell back and water trickled over her cheek. She

lifted up fast enough to cramp her neck. It was like the worst stomach crunch ever.

She heard shuffling noises and looked around for any signs of light. The men grunted and argued and made enough noise to contrast with Pax's complete silence. If he was breathing, he did so without making a sound.

More footsteps and a thud. "Leave it," the deep voice said.

It was another minute before the echo of their footsteps receded. Pax held on through it all. She strained to hear the conversation, but only the ding of the lines on the boat and the shifting of the wooden deck greeted her.

She tried to raise a hand to touch Pax's face, but gravity pushed it down to her stomach again. "I think we're okay."

Pax nodded but didn't pull her up. "Joel?"

"All clear."

Pax slammed his teeth together and yanked her up, bending his arms inch by painful inch. In the last second he went for speed and yanked her harder. Her body slipped up over the lip of the boat. Momentum picked up from there. She flew through the air and crashed into Pax, taking them both down to the deck. She landed in a sprawl over top of him with her legs on each side of his slim hips.

This time she gave in to the need to run her fingers over Pax's cheek. "That weight-lift trick bordered on showing off."

"It was fun."

"Which part, where we almost got discovered, or where I almost ripped your arms out of their sockets?"

He sat up, keeping his hand pressed against her back and easing her along with him. "Both, but now it's time to find a place to sleep tonight."

She straddled his lap, facing him, and had no desire to move, but she would bolt if he answered this question wrong. "Please don't say a boat."

"I have something much better in mind. Should have

started there and skipped the marina, but I promise you'll be happy with the second choice."

If he wasn't talking about a hotel, she might just kill him. "Lead the way."

Chapter Fourteen

It was almost midnight when Bryce stumbled out of his office. He'd been working on a statement about the initial testing of the new program. He had to report to a special Senate subcommittee in private session. He didn't have a choice. This was a command performance requested by members. To be more accurate, ordered.

He stopped in front of Glenn's desk and scanned the papers thrown around in an uncharacteristic mess. Bryce's able assistant's keys sat on the corner with a suit coat resting against the back of the chair. He'd gone somewhere, but Bryce didn't know where.

He started to leave and then stopped. His gaze went back to the papers. Glenn's obsessive tidiness was well-known in the office. Bryce depended on the efficiency that came with having everything in its place. The riot of paperwork didn't fit Glenn at all.

As the boss, Bryce had the right to know about everything that happened in his workspace. That rule was explained in great detail in the employee manual. There could not be any confusion.

Rather than wait and ask for permission, he picked up the documents half tucked under the keyboard and read the name on the top sheet. Kelsey Moore. This was part of her file, which meant Glenn continued to work the sister angle.

Once again Glenn exceeded Bryce's expectations. They'd been unsuccessful so far in tracing the sister's location, but Bryce sensed she was the key and wanted her in front of him as soon as possible, and Glenn ran with the possibility.

Bryce swore under his breath. Looked as if he'd underestimated the coffee girl. She'd gotten out of town at the right time and somehow managed to stay off the grid. Her helper likely had something to do with that. Bryce still worried using the facial recognition program had tipped this Paxton Weeks off, who was even now tracing the personnel file breach back to Kingston. The concern kept Bryce in the office late and had him turning in bed for hours last night.

The only thing that made Bryce question Weeks's role as anything more than a boyfriend was the quiet. There was a way about these things. You tripped into the wrong government file, and the FBI or some agency with a few letters would come banging on the door, asking questions.

Bryce had his excuse ready, but he hadn't had to use it yet. That delay made Bryce question all of his expectations.

The what-if game brought him right back to the file and Kelsey Moore.

Glenn walked into the area with a can of soda in his hand. The space consisted of four half-wall screens and stacks of work. Glen didn't waste his time with personal objects or ridiculous stuffed animals, which Bryce admired. No need to clog up the head with mindless chatter and silly hopes during the workday.

Glenn slid by Bryce and into his chair. "Sir?"

"You should go home. You're no good to me after consecutive nights without sleep."

Glenn tapped on his computer keys to bring up lines of code. "I've developed a matrix to determine where Kelsey might be."

Bryce could answer that question without a fancy computer program. "Wherever Paxton Weeks is we'll find her and, likely, Sean sniffing right behind them both. This is one big circle—Sean to Kelsey to Paxton Weeks."

"I have a list of possibilities."

Bryce took the paper and scanned down the line. "Most of these locations are out of town."

"As you said, she doesn't have a huge number of friends."

Bryce handed the sheet back. "The last line is the answer. She's in Annapolis."

"How do you know?"

This is why he was the boss. Why people like Dan would never ruin him. "I know."

SHE HATED THE WATER.

Pax flicked off the bathroom light with a click and walked down the hallway on the second floor of his brother's row house. Less than a mile from Corcoran headquarters and located in the historic section of Annapolis, the two-story fixer-upper had been Davis's refuge when Lara walked out. Now it was the place they'd build a family and life.

Pax had spent many nights in the house, having dinner and staying over when the idea of the office crash pad had him finding excuses to stay. Not that he needed one. He had a standing invitation by Davis and Lara to move in with them until he got his living situation worked out post-boat destruction. But he didn't want to interrupt. Not when they'd just found each other.

But Davis being Davis, he made sure Pax had a key and knew the security codes. Title to the place was buried under a series of fake corporate names.

Attackers had once come to the door looking for Lara, but those days were behind her. Connor zipped up the security hole so that Davis wouldn't have to move out of the home he loved so much.

Pax trusted the cover to hold. No one could trace this house to him, or to Davis for that matter. He stayed on guard but didn't hunker down by the windows holding his gun. He could relax here.

Tonight he'd showered off the slime from crawling around on the docks and checked in with Connor. But he couldn't wrap his mind around the news of her fears. Traffic and crowds choked him. Open water handed him his breath back.

And she hated the water.

He rolled his sore shoulder back and repeated the idea again in the hope of accepting it better this time. No such luck.

That fear of hers was going to be a problem. It wasn't as if he could ignore that tremble in her voice or the way her moves turned jerky and frantic when she ventured too far to one side of the dock. If the plan was to finish this job and put her back in the coffeehouse and then walk away, all would have been fine. But he'd already decided the only walking he'd be doing was *to* her, not from her.

He turned the corner and came to a slamming halt in the doorway of the guest bedroom. Dresser, bed…and Kelsey. He'd set her up in the master bedroom after changing the sheets and clearing out all evidence of Davis, including his extra watch on the nightstand and pants thrown over the chair in the corner by the window.

She'd slipped down the hall and landed here.

The woman sure knew how to test a man's control.

"Everything okay?" His voice sounded thick and muffled to his ears.

She leaned back stiff-armed with her hands on the bed behind her and her feet on the floor. "Yep."

The outfit she had on slowly killed off the last of his good sense. Tiny straps on the flimsy shirt and shorts that barely reached the middle of her thighs. The pajamas had tiny purple flowers all over them. Probably meant to be sweet, but his gaze kept slipping to the deep V-neck and the shadowed valley between her breasts. The same breasts not bound by a bra.

He had no idea where she'd gotten the set, but he wanted to rip the thin pieces right off her.

The countdown to poor judgment started in his head and radiated right down to his pants. Being alone in the house with her proved tough enough. He'd spent every minute of his quick cold shower imagining her dropping her bath towel and slipping into the cool white sheets he just tucked into the king-size bed in the other room. Seeing her on the small mattress five feet away had his mind scrambling and the alphabet slipping from his mental grasp.

"I thought you were sleeping in the other room." That was the deal he made with his lower half. A short kiss and then hands off.

She smiled as she crossed one leg over the other and let her ankle swing in the air above the plush carpet. "Nope."

"No?" The seductive move sucked all the moisture out of his mouth. He almost swallowed his tongue, which was obvious from how the word slurred.

She shook her head and then patted the space next to her. "Come sit."

She. Was. Killing. Him.

"I'm not sure that's a good idea."

Her head tilted to the side and her long hair brushed over her shoulder, the strands shifting and picking up the light. "Does your leg hurt?"

That was just about the sexiest thing ever. Wait…

"What?" His leg. Everyone wanted to talk about his leg. "No."

Well, not until she mentioned it. Any talk of the wound started the intense throbbing from his knee to his foot. Seemed fair since the rest of him now was, too.

"What about your arms?" she asked.

"My what?"

"You held my dead weight for a long time over the side of that boat."

His shoulder picked that moment to freeze up. "It's fine. You're not heavy."

He groaned inwardly at his lack of smoothness. Yeah, because every woman wanted to hear that sort of thing.

"Aren't you sweet?"

Huh, maybe they did.

She glanced around the room, her focus falling on the photograph on the dresser of Pax with his brother and Lara. "You never told me whose house this is."

He was pretty sure he had, but he welcomed the idle chatter. It gave his brain cells an opportunity to regroup and potentially begin firing again. "Davis and Lara own it."

"And the older woman next door who waved to you from the upstairs window? Wasn't expecting that. Not at midnight."

Pax knew she would be there. She guarded Davis from a distance, believing he was some sort of superspy...and at one time he had been. "Mrs. Winston? She's a very nice and slightly nosy neighbor. Davis watches over her and vice versa."

And Pax had no idea why they were talking about the neighborhood. Not when Kelsey had pulled the drapes and turned on the light on the far bedside table, casting the entire room in a soft glow. Not when she sat like that and he could barely stand.

"Mrs. Winston just sits in that window?"

"It's a long story, but she played a significant role in helping Davis handle the men after Lara."

Kelsey's ankle continued to wave back and forth. "Really?"

Pax leaned against the door frame. No way was he going an inch farther into that room. "Don't let the white hair and petite frame fool you. She possesses a lot of strength and a loyalty streak for Davis."

But whom was he telling? Kelsey greeted customers with a smile and filled out her blue work apron in ways Pax always found interesting. Who would have guessed she'd have a stronger will than him?

Her hands slipped against the comforter and her back dipped closer to the mattress. "Are you coming to bed?"

He ignored the way she said that. The way her body moved, so sleek it made him crazy. "Kelsey, if I get on that mattress we are not going to get an hour of rest before dawn."

Her eyebrow lifted. "And?"

"You need sleep. Hell, I need sleep." His mind went to the condoms he'd thrown in the nightstand right before his shower. He chalked it up to a healthy dose of wishful thinking.

Truth was he put them in the bag back at team headquarters and hid them in this room when he'd handed the bag over to her twenty minutes ago. Didn't want her to find them and for him to come off as too sleazy or presumptuous.

Protecting a woman was mandatory for him. He viewed that as the man's job in the bedroom and out. But he grabbed the packets back when he thought the terror of the night was ebbing and they could spend a few hours winding down in the most interesting ways. Then he'd subjected her to terror-by-water, somehow got through it and decided she'd had enough for one day.

"Is that what you want?" One leg slid off the other and she curled them up under her as she lay on her side with her head resting on her hand. "For me to go into the other room and leave you alone?"

Still killing him.

But why lie? "No."

She smiled in that way women did when the men in their lives strayed into their sexy little mind traps. "Then come to bed."

He debated the pros and cons, thought about every angle and heard Connor's arguments running in his head. That took all of two seconds. Pax spent the rest of the time on his walk to the mattress, imagining how good her bare skin would feel against his.

He stopped at the edge of the bed and skimmed his fingers along her side, over her hip and onto her upper thigh. "You are so beautiful. From the first time I saw you, I wanted you."

"My hair was in a ponytail and my feet ached from waiting on the rush hour crowd." She slipped her hand over his and brought his palm back up to her waist. "Yeah, I remember the first time you came in, too. All hot and sexy with that five o'clock shadow and the faded jeans."

Now that sounded promising…and hard to resist no matter how chivalrous he intended to be. "Sexy, huh?"

"You can't be that clueless." She shifted to her back as she pressed his hand against her bare stomach. "You do own a mirror, right?"

Physical looks weren't on his radar. Hers, yes. His? No.

He sat down next to her, and she scooted over to make room for him by her hip. There were so many things he wanted to do. So many places he wanted to touch. He settled for lowering his head and pressing his mouth against hers.

Her soft lips opened under his as her hand slid up his thigh. Hot and wet, he kissed her, letting her feel the buildup of need that had been haunting him all day. Electricity shot between them and his heart smacked against his breastbone. The kiss went to his head and then spread through the rest of him. The intoxicating touch made him wonder how he'd waited until now to have her.

But he wanted more. His mouth traveled over her chin to the thin line of her neck. Every inch of her tasted sweet and smooth. His fingers brushed up her stomach to the underside of her breast. He cupped her, caressed her. He had to see her.

In one swift move he had her shirt up and off. With infinite care, he traced his finger around her bare breasts to the center. Fire raced through him a second later as her back lifted off the bed and her arms wrapped around his neck. He touched her everywhere. With his mouth and his hands. His fingertips rubbed against her nipples as he marveled at how her body reacted to his.

There wasn't a breath of air between them. He sprawled over her, careful not to crush her under his weight. Up on his elbows, he could see her expressive face and watch her skin flush as his hand slipped under the waistband of her shorts. He kept going until he felt her heat and wetness against his skin.

Never breaking contact, he reached out for the nightstand drawer. His fingers fumbled on the knob and slapped against the top. With a yank the drawer came out in a rush and hung from his hand. He grabbed for a condom and then let the wooden drawer crash to the floor.

She never stopped kissing him. Her mouth skimmed along his throat as her hands rolled his tee in a ball before wrenching it off. Skin hit skin and everything inside him tightened and coiled. He wanted to rush and get inside her, but he needed to slow down. He had to make this good for her.

He thought about kissing down her belly and tasting the very heat of her, but she had other ideas. Her fingers went to his zipper, and it ripped through the room as she lowered it.

One minute his erection was cramped in his tight jeans. The next she freed him, sliding her hand inside and closing her fist over him.

His mind spun, and all intelligent thought raced from his

brain. His concern centered on stripping her naked and rolling around in those sheets with her. They could sleep later.
Right now he needed her.

When he lowered his mouth to hers again, he felt a tug in
his hand and a scrape against his palm. The condom slipped
out of his grasp. He wanted to lift his head and see what happened, but a tearing sound ripped through the room. She had
the condom out. Then she rolled it on him.

His brain screamed for him to slow down and savor, but he
was too far gone. The combination of her tongue against his
and her hand moving up and down his erection made slamming the brakes on impossible. Instinct took over. His fingers
met hers as he helped her fit the condom to him.

Then his fingers slipped inside her. Her thighs opened on
each side of his hip and her hips bucked against him. He slid
into her, back and forth, harder with each push.

"Faster." She whispered the word right before she bit down
on his ear.

He blocked out everything but the unsteady pulse of her
breathing and the slide of skin against skin. Blood hammered
as it rushed to his ears and drummed there.

A mix of excitement and need spun inside him. The churning revved as he pressed in and out. Light exploded in his
brain just as her head rocked against her mattress. She was
sexy and vibrant, and when her fingernails dug into his back,
he knew what he found with her was more than a onetime
thing.

Chapter Fifteen

The next afternoon Joel stopped clicking on his keyboard and threw his fists in the air in triumph. "He's good but I'm better."

Connor leaned over Kelsey's shoulder and dropped a plate of premade deli sandwiches on the table. "A general topic would be helpful."

"And some idea about the 'who' in that sentence would be nice." Since this was the third time Joel had declared his brilliance during the past hour, and she still didn't know why, she didn't get too excited. Instead, she picked through the tuna choices until she found turkey. Boss or not, the man sure knew how to order food.

Joel spun his chair around to face the conference room table. His gaze switched from Kelsey to Pax, who sat across from her. "I traced the check on Pax's file to its source. As we thought, a facial recognition program using a video of Pax pinged the DOD file. Took twenty hours of nonstop work, but I made the connections."

She almost hated to ask a simple question when Joel's huge smile suggested he was pretty proud of his accomplishment. She just wished she knew what that accomplishment was. "How exactly?"

Joel waved her off. "Trade secrets."

She would have bet money he'd say that. Even Pax chuckled at the obvious response. She went with an eye roll and sarcastic tone. "Well, of course it is."

"Not from your boss it isn't." Connor sat down next to her with his ever-present cup of coffee. "Spill it."

"I'll fill in the details later, but by tapping into the FBI's database on—"

Connor groaned. "Forget it. I don't want to know. If you skip this part I can maintain plausible deniability when I get called into the FBI to explain, and I'm betting I will."

Pax, who had been quiet since they came back to headquarters at Connor's request an hour ago, leaned back in his chair. "Was there a point to all the celebration?"

"Bryce Kingston. To be more specific, or less specific, depending on how you look at it, Kingston's office. The security breach about Pax's identity was initiated there. We thought so and now we have proof."

Joel didn't say "busted," but for some reason she thought it was implied.

"So he did see me with Pax outside my shop." She'd expected this answer, but knowing someone watched her every move made her want to shower for a decade.

"Can you pinpoint which desk or computer? I want to tag Bryce with this but it could be someone under him. Someone he will throw under the bus when the time comes." Connor scooped up a sandwich and put it on the napkin in front of him. He didn't eat it. Just let it sit there.

"No one is that good," Joel said.

She glanced at Pax and spied him looking at her. The smile spread across her lips before she could stop it. The rush of heat to her cheeks was harder to hide. She settled for holding a coffee mug to her mouth, forgetting that it was empty. She hoped Connor didn't pick up on that fact.

But sitting there trying to act cool and together after spending hours last night rolling across the guest room bed with Pax proved difficult. Being with him topped all her expectations and blew away her dreams. She wanted the real version and now that she had him, she couldn't go back to pretending he was nothing more than an attractive and unforgettable customer.

They had a bond, strong and sexy. He calmed her ragged nerves even as he set her blood on fire. The combination of protective and caring felled her. He'd spent the entire night touching her.

Even when the lovemaking died down and they drifted off to sleep, his hand rested against her stomach or her shoulder or her back. She'd felt his breath and his smooth touch. He continued all morning with a brush against her arm here and a hand through her hair there.

She'd been relieved when he took the chair across from her at the office. Her body was so sensitized to him that any close proximity might result in her losing her mind, ignoring the crowd and climbing right on top of him and showering him with another round of kisses. She doubted that little item number was on Connor's daily agenda. Turned out sitting across from Pax and looking deep into his eyes wasn't any easier on her control.

"So, genius, what does this tell us?" Pax asked.

"Kingston is hacking into your life, which means he's likely the person sending the attackers after you and Kelsey."

She understood the math here. One plus one and all that, but the bottom line didn't fit together for her. "He's a businessman."

Connor winced. "That's a naive response."

The words didn't offend her. The comment was more about filling her in than talking down to her. She could sense that in the even tone and constant eye contact. "Do you honestly think he would kill me to keep some information I don't even understand quiet? If Joel is right, Kingston has seen

Pax's government file, and you think that's not a deterrent? It would be a big risk to take Pax on."

He nodded. "Thank you."

"Bryce Kingston's potential take on this project is in the billions, and that's just to start," Connor said.

True, that was a pretty big reward. Maybe even worth the risk. She learned from her father what some men would do for money—marry, abandon their children, break the law, wrongly accuse old friends, lie about everything.

The list went on and on. "Okay, admittedly that's big money."

Joel tapped his pen against his open palm. "It looks like Sean broke through Kingston's security system and took the data, which means Kingston could be looking at a lifetime ban in government contracting for failing to oversee the secure program."

There was one factor that could save them all…at least she hoped that was true. Maybe they could fix whatever Sean did before it totally blew up.

Where before she'd blindly say and think Sean could fend for himself, now she knew she'd step in and help if she could. Whatever blood bond they shared ensured at least that much. She craved more, wanted what Pax had with Davis, but she doubted that could ever be.

"But the government wants the product." She didn't bother with the question. She skipped right to a fact she knew from Connor's earlier briefing.

"Sometimes in these things another company suddenly has the R&D to launch a prototype at the same time, and the government goes with them instead."

That sounded bad. Like, lost-their-leverage bad. "So now what?"

"We pay Mr. Kingston a visit." Pax swiveled in his chair

and stood up. Wherever he was going became a memory when Connor started talking.

He pointed at her and then Pax. "Not you. Or her."

She was mostly okay with that last part.

Pax leaned across the table. "I need to question this Kingston guy."

"He's digging into your background," Connor said. "We're not making it easier for him to find you."

Pax's hands found his hips and his frown cut through his words. "He needs to know I'm not afraid and will most certainly come after him if he doesn't back off."

"He'll get that message. I will see to it." Connor's voice remained even but the intensity of his stare did not ease.

Kelsey's gaze bounced around the room as she watched the men argue. Joel stayed out of this part, but from the way he sat on the edge of his chair, he was no less engaged. Part of her wanted to crawl under the table.

She sat there and listened to Pax insist on his right to rush into danger. The idea of him being a target—again—because of her family made her put down the turkey sandwich. No way could she eat now.

Pax knocked his fists against the table. "I want to be there."

Of course he did. He wouldn't sit this one out. She knew any mention of his injury would have that tick in his cheek snapping. Trying to help him could ratchet up his defense shield and guarantee he stepped further into danger.

That left few options for her. She wanted to hide in a closet, but when it came to keeping Pax safe she was prepared to come out fighting. No one touched him. She understood his training and believed he could handle almost anything, but that didn't mean she could sit back and agree to let it happen.

"You and Kelsey need to be in hiding, making it difficult

for anyone to get to either of you. Flaunting you in front of Kingston is not the answer." Connor shot Pax a man-to-man serious expression. "It also jeopardizes the team."

She liked the way that sounded. No way could Pax argue with that logic. "You should have led with that argument."

Joel's pen tapping picked up speed. "Not to question Connor's authority here or risk Kelsey's wrath, but I think Pax should go."

She seriously considered punching the man, or at least hitting him with the keyboard he loved so much. "Why?"

"Pax's presence will shake Kingston up. That's our only chance here. Catch him off guard and measure the reaction. We bring in government officials and start asking questions, and this whole thing will shut down without us knowing who is after Kelsey or Sean's piece in this."

"Meaning too many loose ends," Connor mumbled.

Pax snapped his fingers a few times and pointed at Joel. "Exactly my point."

She knew that was a bad sign. Pax now had an ally. They'd work on Connor until he caved, and he sounded right on the edge already. The man was strong but not stupid. If Pax agreed to take on the danger and it meant an end to the case, she suspected Connor would allow it. That would leave her out as the lone dissenter.

Working against Pax didn't appeal to her.

Neither did being left behind.

She sighed at Pax, letting him know she didn't appreciate the direction of the conversation. "You're not going to back down, are you?"

"If it helps, he's not in charge here," Connor said.

But she knew Pax. If he wanted this to happen, it would happen. That meant she had to tamp down the ball of anxiety boiling in her stomach and get on the right side of this. The right side in Pax's view, that is.

"I agree with Joel." It actually hurt a little to say the words.

"You do?" Joel and Connor asked at the same time.

Pax's question came in slower. It carried a hint of disbelief and wariness in his eyes. "Really?"

She bit back the fear and dread. Pressed all those knee-buckling doubts out of her head and dived in. "You guys do this work all the time and hang out with each other. You don't know how intimidating you are. Having Pax there, issuing a direct threat to Bryce Kingston—"

He cleared his throat. "And I do intend to do that."

"—will make an impression."

The words rang out and then silence. Joel smiled but Pax scowled at her. Connor was the mystery. He sat with an elbow balanced on the chair's armrest and stared her down. After a few seconds, he wiped his fingers around the corners of his mouth and stared at the table.

Finally he looked up, pinning her with his blue-eyed gaze. "Fine."

Pax shifted his weight and had them all looking in his direction. "Good, but she stays here."

"No." That was it. Connor dropped the verbal bomb and stopped talking.

Confusion and something that looked suspiciously like guilt shone in Pax's eyes. "Connor, wait a second."

But Connor was already off and running to the next thing. She could almost see him making the calculations in his head. When the full force of his stare bore into her, she had to sit back in her chair. The leather squeaked under her butt.

"You both come along and we go for the big hit. We let Bryce know he has a breach and we're aware of it." Connor's gaze flicked to Pax for a second. "Seeing the two of you should throw him off, or at least convince him to make a play. Then we've got him."

She wasn't completely sure she'd won the argument. If

she had her way she'd have her hand in Pax's as they waltzed out the front door and back to bed. Her motivation was not a mystery. Connor's was not as clear. "You're doing it because I said so?"

Connor shrugged. "We're trying it because you made a good argument, and so did Joel. We go in, spook Bryce and then follow."

"We need to talk about the specifics and Kelsey's role, which should be nothing." Pax's growl didn't leave any question about his thoughts on the new operation. He planned to talk Connor out of this plan.

She was just as determined to make sure Pax lost that argument. Dirty tricks, cheating. Whatever it took, she would be by his side when they all confronted this Kingston guy. They needed a show of force, and she would make sure they gave it to him. She needed this over, and whatever they deemed the fastest way to do that was fine with her.

"I'm thinking Connor made his decision and we're a go. I'll start working on logistics." Joel turned back to his computers.

"I just hope I'm right." Connor mumbled the words.

She heard them only because they sat a few feet apart. That hard-to-swallow thing came back. "We all do."

SEAN DISCONNECTED THE call and put his father's cell down on the kitchen counter. The small thud echoed through the big empty space. He remembered the weeks of construction when his mom updated this room years ago. Dark custom-made cabinets and a huge island made from a slab of granite his father insisted had cost more than college tuition.

The space had the best of everything. Never mind no one actually cooked in it. Not anymore. The maid once made a few meals per week, but the family had always been the eat-out type. Dining at "the club" was one of his mother's favorite things.

Now his father rarely ventured out of the caretaker's cottage on the property. He lingered there or in the massive master suite that took up half of the second floor and contained more square feet than most family houses.

He picked this moment to shuffle into the room. The golf shoes clicked against the tile as he slid his feet across the floor, probably trying not to trip.

Ice clinked in the glass that he rotated in his hand. He'd shifted to bourbon right after lunch. "What did she say?"

"I couldn't reach her." And that made him nervous. Kelsey had a business and was always there, or that's what she claimed the last time they'd talked. He'd been looking for work and wanted to talk with her. She didn't have time.

"Try again." His father lifted his other hand to reveal the crystal decanter in it. "I'll listen in."

That would not help the situation at all. Sean knew that much. Not answering the phone pointed to the bigger sibling problem. One he didn't think he could dissect on top of everything else going on. "She's not picking up."

His father dropped the bottle on the counter. Then the glass hit with a hard ding right before he balanced his open palms against the island. The fingernail tapping against the stone started a second later. "We need her attention."

Sean wondered when this had become a "we" situation. "I'm not sure this is the right way to go. I mean, maybe the answer is to talk with Kingston or someone like the FBI. Come clean."

The space between his father's shoulders stiffened. He glanced up, not lifting his head the whole way but staring at Sean over the top of his glasses. "You are going to stick with the plan, deliver the goods and then you can go wherever you want."

"It's not that simple."

"Which is why I am helping you." The older man walked around the edge of the island to stand right in front of Sean. "Tell your sister you're in trouble and she needs to come here with the box. Immediately."

"Why would she?"

"She's soft. It's one of her many weaknesses."

"But someone could follow her." Sean shifted his weight and sat on a high bar stool at the breakfast bar. Anything to put a bit of distance between his body and the wall of fury coming at him from his father.

The older man's lips screwed up in a look of distaste. "That's not your concern."

But it was. Being on the run helped Sean understand that. Everything unfolding now could be traced back to his decisions. To his actions. He'd sent the box to Kelsey because in a world filled with friends more concerned with the kind of car they drove than what was happening at Sean's office, she was the only person he trusted. The realization stunned him. They rarely spoke and never saw each other, but he knew she was the one he could confide in.

His father's mouth fell and his expression turned strangely blank. "We need the documents."

This time Sean couldn't resist getting clarification. "We?"

"Yes, son." The older man jammed his finger against the granite with each word he spoke. "When you jumped that fence out front you made this my problem, and I'm going to fix it."

"I can handle it."

"If that were true, you would have sent the documents to me in the first place and not to Kelsey. She's useless. Getting her to hand them over will take quite a bit of convincing. The kind of incentive you may not like."

The words scraped against the inside of Sean's brain as a fissure of wariness shot through him. "They're safe with her."

"Safety isn't the issue."

It was Sean's only concern, but his father's mind clearly wandered elsewhere. "What is the issue?"

"Making money." His father grabbed the scruff of Sean's neck and shook him. The words spit into Sean's ear.

Sean shook him off. "What are you doing?"

"Knocking some sense into you." His father stalked to the other side of the island and yanked on a drawer. He pulled out a gun and dropped it on the counter with a clank.

Sean blinked and shook his head. It took a second for the weapon to register. When the barrel and trigger came into focus, he jumped off the stool and eased away from the kitchen island. "Why do you have that?"

"Insurance."

"For what?"

His father frowned as if he thought the answer was obvious. "To make sure I get my way."

Everyone talked about how difficult Sandy Moore could be. Friends insisted his personality and not actual fraud led to the criminal charges. He was a target because of how he dealt with people and the enemies he'd made. With his ego, he did nothing to move the bull's-eye off his chest.

Sean had believed it all. He'd once ignored Kelsey's claims about the checks in their father's desk drawer and his ironfisted control over money. Sean wrote all the arguments off as whining from the oldest and less successful child.

But a gun and very real threats to use it ventured well beyond difficult. Blew right past it, actually. This wasn't just about money. His father seemed prepared to engage in needless violence.

Not to protect them. No, to get his way, even if he had to turn it on his blood relatives to do it.

A gun, the implied threats, the spitting disdain for even the mention of Kelsey's name. Sean studied his father's face and saw, for the first time, the wild craziness in his eyes. It was possible he'd finally driven over the edge of reason.

And now he had a gun instead of checkbook and other people's money to play with.

Sean's gaze slipped from his father to the gun as he waited for a chance to grab it. But his father never lifted his hand. "Dad, I think we need—"

"That's what you and I are going to do, Sean. Make money. It's either that or we're going to have a problem." His fingers tightened on the weapon. "Do you understand me?"

All too clearly. Standing there with fear pinching his neck and squeezing the nerve until a headache pounded behind his eyes, Sean saw it all unfold. The end played out in his head. Irrational thought had replaced his father's once-strong business sense. He focused on revenge and his sense of entitlement. He'd all but bought into his own deluded argument of being the victim in a press and prosecution witch hunt.

No doubt about it. Sean had gone to the exact wrong place for help, and now Kelsey could pay the price.

Chapter Sixteen

The call came on a Friday morning. Bryce sat in the claustrophobic, windowless room in a nondescript office building near the Severn River and just outside of Annapolis. He'd been summoned for an emergency meeting about his baby, the Signal Reconnaissance Program. The contracting officer mentioned security concerns initiated by someone at the Pentagon. Bryce had spent the morning preparing for the hours of questioning.

This had to be about Sean Moore. Everything lately revolved around Sean Moore and his deception.

The whole fiasco landed Bryce in the firing line of the very military officials he'd been courting for more than two years. A target now covered his back.

So much for thinking Dan would make things run more smoothly. Little did he know that the script Bryce had invented for this meeting and the paperwork trail he created back at the office placed all responsibility for Sean's activities on Dan's lap.

But none of that mattered while Bryce paced the small office. There was nothing plush about the space. He had a metal desk and a cheap chair. Glenn had been banished to the hallway to wait. Why the officials wanted him separated from Glenn still wasn't clear to Bryce.

The admirals and government contracting officials who

called the meeting were here for a presentation of some sort
unrelated to Bryce or his company. Bryce's job consisted of
standing there without complaint.

The rapid knocking on the door broke through his brewing
fury. The door opened only a few inches, and Glenn peeked
in. His usually tan face had taken on a white cast.

But it was the interruption that surprised Bryce. "What
are you doing?"

"You have unexpected guests." Glenn's eyes were huge
and his fingers wrapped around the door in a tight clench.

His assistant had never been one for dramatics. He walked
into meetings with powerful people and gave off an air of
calm. Today he looked ready to break. And his comment
made no sense.

"Guests? This isn't a hotel. Are you talking about our
meeting?"

"No. These are other people who insist on seeing you."

Bryce was not in the mood for games. He'd almost reached
his end on this top-secret nonsense. He deserved more respect than to be shuffled into the equivalent of a cell by a
low-level employee. "Tell security not to let the people in the
building. If they want to see me, they can make an appoint-
ment back at our offices like everyone else."

"They're already out here in the hall."

Bryce remembered the scanners and metal detectors. The
process of getting guest passes took a half hour. Even then,
Bryce had to walk with an escort and stay in a strict zone
that included only a long white hallway filled with closed
doors. "How did that happen?"

The office door pushed open and a man in his late thirties
walked in. Dark hair, muscular build and no one Bryce ever
remembered seeing before. He'd memorize his face but he
had a feeling he'd never find a thread on the guy.

But that didn't mean Bryce would accept scare tactics. "What do you want?"

The man stepped just inside the door and stopped. His shoulders blocked the view of Glenn. Blocked out everything.

"I was determined to see you." That's all he said. He dropped the statement and then let it sit there.

"Who are you?" Bryce did a visual scan for weapons while he asked. They were there. He could sense it. The guy had a retired military look to him—tough, no-nonsense and trained.

"My name isn't important and not something you're privy to anyway." The man steadied his stance, inching his legs apart and clasping his hands behind his back. "You're asking the wrong questions. You should be concerned with what I want, not who I am."

Bryce leaned to the side to get a better view of Glenn. Eye contact proved impossible since Glenn's attention stayed on something behind him in the hallway. Bryce didn't even want to know who or what that could be. Making the distress call too late wouldn't help them.

Time to ask for reinforcements. "Call security."

Glenn mumbled something and then spoke louder. "Sir, I think—"

"Don't." Gone was the anger at being yanked around. A real concern about safety and this unknown man's connections for getting in here took over inside Bryce. "Do it now, Glenn."

The unknown man held up his hand. "Wait a minute there, Glenn."

Bryce swallowed back old fears and centered his will on staying calm. "You sticking around will make it easier for the police when they get here, but you may wish to play this whole scene a little smarter than that."

"Maybe I can help clear this up." Another man stepped into the room, pushing Glenn out of the doorway as he went.

Bryce didn't need an introduction this time. He'd seen that face for days on his computer screen and agonized over the accidental trip into the man's confidential government file. Paxton Weeks, one of the people Bryce had been tracking and potentially a very dangerous man.

Small space. Men with training and government protection. Bryce didn't know what kind of meeting this was, but he started to have the gnawing fear he wouldn't survive it.

In an act that could be called only bravery, Glenn moved around the two bigger men and stood in the middle of the small room. "Sir, what do you want me to do?"

Now that Bryce had some idea of the players, security seemed unnecessary. These two had whatever access they needed to be in the room, and all the yelling wouldn't drive them out. "You can leave, Glenn."

"Yes. Goodbye, Glenn." A woman's voice issued the dismissal right before she stepped out from behind Weeks. "I think you know who I am."

Kelsey Moore.

After days of useless searching, she'd walked right into range. Bryce fought back the urge to reach out and grab her. The two bodyguards would probably kill him if he tried. "What is this about?"

Paxton shifted, subtle but definite, to block most of Kelsey's body from view. The sign was clear. Any attack on her would have to go through him. "We know about your search for my work file. Big mistake, by the way."

The entire meeting agenda crystallized. This wasn't about Sean. It was about Bryce's own search. Not that he could admit that. "I don't know what you're talking about."

"The facial recognition software. I hear the NSA is upset about that breach, by the way."

The ball of anxiety bouncing around Bryce's stomach picked up in speed. "I create programs of that sort. That is not a secret."

Paxton kept up his rapid-fire questioning. "And how do you explain the men you sent to Kelsey's house?"

The ball shot around until it choked Bryce. "I'm afraid your paranoia is out of control."

"You have one chance to come clean." The unknown man made the comment without moving an inch.

"Who are you again?" Whatever his name, the guy seemed to be in charge and more than happy to let Paxton launch into an abusive battle.

"You still don't need to know my name," the unknown man said.

Paxton walked to the other side of the desk and balanced his hands on it. The move put him far too close for Bryce's comfort. This one likely wouldn't need a weapon. If the muscles and furious glare were any indication, he'd break bones first and ask questions later.

"You made a mistake." Paxton's voice dropped with red-hot fury.

There were too many mistakes for Bryce to count at this point. All those old insecurities rushed back on him. He'd built a company and commanded respect from hundreds of employees with impressive credentials. None of that would save him if Paxton decided to unload.

Bryce crossed his arms over his chest and held his ground. "Explain all of your accusations."

"You wanted your property back from Sean Moore. Understandable, but you went too far. You invaded Kelsey's privacy, you put her in danger and you didn't stop even after the first wave of attackers fell." Paxton made a tsk-tsk sound. "I can't allow that."

That was the second reference to attackers. "I don't know what you're talking about with the danger part."

This time Bryce wasn't lying. The surveillance and Sean. Bryce got that. The talk of attackers didn't fit at all. If someone had physically gone after Sean and his sister, it wasn't Bryce. Which made him wonder what and who else was in play.

One minute he was standing there and the next Paxton reached across the desk and grabbed a fist full of shirt. Paxton tightened his fist as the words shot out of him. "I'm done with you."

Bryce struggled to break the hold but the guy didn't budge. With one hand on his tie, Bryce tried to keep his collar from cutting off his breath. "Hey, you can't—"

"Oh, I assure you I can."

Clutching at his shirt and shuffling his feet, Bryce conducted a frantic scan of the room. The other guy didn't show any emotion. Kelsey bit down on her lip. She was his way in. A regular woman with a menial job. She wouldn't let the bruiser kill him.

"Lady, come on."

"You wrecked my building and my work. I won't even mention what you did to my sense of security." She shook her head. "Don't expect me to help you."

"I didn't do anything but tap into cameras."

Paxton shook Bryce until he coughed out a gasp.

Finally, the quiet leader spoke up. "Mr. Kingston can't help us if he's dead."

The strangling sensation disappeared as Paxton shoved against Bryce's chest. He landed in the chair, rolling until it slammed against the back wall. "What's wrong with you?"

"Talk."

Bryce stared at three furious glares. Flushed faces and stiff bodies. They knew too much yet in some ways nothing at all. He had two choices—deny or come clean on the parts he could control. "Sean stole proprietary information from me. I tracked him down and that led me to family members. My investigator went to Ms. Moore's shop but there was a gas leak. End of story."

"Why did you send people to kill me?" Kelsey's voice shook as she yelled the question.

Reference number three to physical violence, and the source for the accusation wasn't any clearer to Bryce. "Tell me what happened."

"You're saying it wasn't you." The leader issued the comment as a challenge.

"I tapped into security cameras. I admit that. The rest has nothing to do with me."

"Who else is involved in this project and the problem with Sean?"

"Dan Breckman, my assistant. The person who administered Sean's lie detector test." The list was small but Dan occupied the top slot. For the first time Bryce wondered if Dan had been working a different angle the entire time. "If you're talking about who knows the program Sean worked on, there are many people with access and information, including other employees, the contracting officers, people in the Pentagon who pushed for this program and a long list of competitors who are furious I got there first."

Paxton and Kelsey shared a look.

The leader was the first to fill the silence. "But you only played with some cameras."

Bryce's heartbeat sped up. He suddenly felt as if he was in a fight for his life and losing ground with each second. "That's right."

The leader shrugged. "We'll see what the investigators think."

The blood drained out of Bryce's head. He wanted to stand up, but he didn't think his legs would hold him. "Excuse me?"

"They're ripping apart your office and searching through your computers right now," Paxton said.

The weight of the past few weeks crashed down on Bryce. He couldn't breathe and tried to swallow. "You can't—"

The leader took out his phone and gave it a quick check. "We're not."

"Apparently you upset some folks in the Pentagon." Paxton's smile took on a feral quality. "By the way, they want you to stay here because they have some questions for you."

They headed for the door, pushing Glenn aside as they went. "Wait. Where are you going?"

"Is something wrong?" Dan's voice.

Shock jabbed into Bryce. Dan…here? Bryce's head spun. Something was happening. Something huge and out of control, and Dan sat at the center of it all. Bryce wanted to lunge across the desk and strangle the guy. He was smart to hide behind Paxton Weeks.

Bryce struggled to his feet, ignoring the dizziness that assailed his brain. "What are you doing here?"

"I got a call to come in."

"Apparently this is the place to be," Paxton said before he walked out, taking Dan with him.

"Have a good afternoon." The leader made the comment over his shoulder but stopped when he hit the doorway and then turned back around. "Oh, and, we'll talk again soon."

PAX DROVE DOWN the warehouse access road. Beige buildings lined each side, and only a stray car or two passed them on the opposite side. They were in the middle of a low-density business park, one that had been mostly cleared out in anticipation of the meeting with Bryce.

It took a massive amount of work to get all the players

in place and convince the officials at the Pentagon to assist. Finding out one of their prized programs was in peril helped. Having Connor lead the operation got the rest done.

Even now he sat in the backseat with Kelsey. She gnawed on her lip, and he constantly searched the area as it passed by the car window.

Pax looked over their heads and glanced in the rearview mirror for the hundredth time. The blue sedan swung out between two garage buildings. For minutes the sedan followed Pax's car. When he turned, the sedan turned shortly thereafter.

To make sure this was the sign he wanted, Pax made a sudden turn and skimmed a narrow alley between loading docks and stopped trailers. A second later the sedan followed.

Bingo.

"We have company." As much as Pax enjoyed the words and when a plan came together, he hated having her in the car. He wanted her at home and safe. His home, even though he didn't currently have one of those.

"About time," Joel mumbled over the comm.

Kelsey tore her gaze away from the window and the bare landscape outside. "We want company?"

Pax watched her, impressed that she didn't fidget or break into outright panic, both of which would be expected from any civilian in this situation. Instead, she sat there, twisting her long tee between two fingers even as her voice stayed steady. "We want to stop the car behind us and figure out who sent it."

Her gaze met his and she frowned. "Isn't it obvious? Bryce Kingston."

Connor made a noise somewhere between a grunt and an exhale. "He'd be too smart to sic someone on our tail now. After that meeting he knows we're on to him. By now he has a crowd of people shooting questions at him. There is nothing he can hide, and he doesn't have as much as a pencil with him in that room. No phone and no way to call his cronies and send them after us."

Impressive explanation but Pax thought Connor used way too many words to get the point across. "Besides all that, he's too busy sitting in that room trying to figure out how to cover his—"

"Watch the road." Connor struck the back of the seat with the heel of his hand. "Turn up here."

Dirt kicked up under the tires as they moved off the paved stretch to a smaller access way. The deeper into the area they drove, winding around warehouses and loading docks, the more remote it became. They could be in Arizona or Kentucky from all they could see.

"This looks like an abandoned alley," Kelsey said as she swiveled her head to see in front of the car.

"It is." Connor tapped his ear. "Joel, you ready?"

"I'm watching."

The adrenaline rush of the chase gave way to a blinding fear she'd be hurt. Pax blinked his eyes to bring his concentration back to the task ahead of him. Seeing her in the backseat acting as if they were on a sightseeing trip didn't do anything to ease the tightening of his nerves.

He shot her a look from the rearview mirror. "Get down on the floor and do not move until I tell you it's okay."

Worry made his words gruff but he didn't apologize. She needed to know this was serious and she shouldn't fool around with any rescue antics.

She nodded. "Right."

This was not his first day with this woman. No way was he falling for that noncommittal response. "No, I know that means you'll do whatever you want. Tell me you'll do what I say."

Her teeth clenched together. "Fine."

Joel laughed over the comm. "I'm not convinced that's a better answer."

"Turn right and slow down." Connor barked out directions as he shifted his weight closer to the door and brought out his gun. "How many do we have?"

Pax squinted for a better view against the afternoon sun. "Just one guy that I can see."

"Get ready." Connor slipped his hand under the door handle as Kelsey ducked.

As soon as he made the turn, Pax slammed on the brakes. The tires skidded and squealed as he cut the wheel to the right. Momentum took them sliding sideways. Industrial trash bins stood in their path, but the car stopped in a cloud of dust right before they crashed into the metal.

The car behind them didn't fare as well. The brakes grinded and the car spun. There was a loud bang as the back tire blew out.

Pax and Connor jumped out of the car, guns aimed, and ran for the attacker's sedan. The driver's hands flew around and his concentration centered on the car. The front end slammed into a green trash bin but not hard enough for the air bag to pop. Even stopped, the driver continued to wrestle with the steering wheel and rev the engine as he floored the gas.

Not that he was going anywhere. Joel's car had him penned in at the back and his shot took care of the tire. Connor and Pax took care of the rest.

"Raise your hands and get out of the car." Connor yelled the order.

The driver's head shot up. He glanced around, as if noticing for the first time the people closing in on him.

With a final look at the car to ensure Kelsey hadn't sat up, Pax circled the front of the sedan and opened the driver's-side door.

The man kept his hands in the air as ordered. "Hey, I was just driving to work."

"Sure you were." Pax grabbed the guy out of the car by his collar and threw him up against the side of the car. While Connor covered him, Pax conducted a pat down. He found the gun in the first pocket he checked. "You plan on shooting some trucks today?"

"I have a license for that."

Connor scoffed. "You'll have a lot of time to explain."

The car door opened and Kelsey stepped out. "We okay?"

Pax swore under his breath. Then he let out another stream much louder. "Get back in the car."

"Fine, but I want to go home."

That made two of them.

Chapter Seventeen

It had been hours since the scene with Bryce Kingston and the car. Connor and some friends from government agencies Kelsey didn't even know existed were interviewing the driver and Bryce Kingston. Kelsey had showered and eaten and then showered again. For whatever reason and despite the humid summer night, her skin refused to warm. She trembled and shook, trying to calm her nerves before her teeth chattered and she really embarrassed herself.

Being with Pax, surrounded by his support, helped. Walking around the hardwood floors in thick athletic socks did, too.

Pax stuck his head in the master bedroom. "You find a sweatshirt?"

She'd ventured into the room when he suggested she check for a sweater or something. She hadn't worked up the nerve to open a drawer yet. "I'm not really comfortable shuffling through your sister-in-law's personal items."

He leaned against the door frame. "I'd rather you touch her underwear than me."

That did sound kind of awful. "Good point."

She opened the top drawer and saw stacks of silky underwear. Yeah, Kelsey could see where touching those might emotionally cripple Pax. Shifting lacy things to the side and around, she looked for anything heavier to wear, but nothing stuck out. She repeated the search with the next drawer down.

"You did great today." The smile sounded in his voice.

The rough, husky tone made her all shivery, but she may as well tell him the truth rather than let him think she was some kind of tough girl. "I wanted to throw up the entire time."

He laughed. "That's probably normal."

She stopped shuffling T-shirts and shorts and stared up at him. "Have you ever thrown up?"

"When I had the flu."

"You're hysterical." Her hand hit on a rough edge and something sliced the top of her finger. She yelped as she pulled her hand back. Red drops oozed on the tip of her finger.

A paper cut.

He was beside her in a shot. He cradled her hand in his and studied the minor wound with great seriousness. "What happened?"

"Attacked by an envelope."

"What?"

She pulled out the offending stack. "These."

He loomed over Kelsey's shoulder. "Weird. Why would Lara keep letters in there?"

Men. If Kelsey weren't so tired she'd roll her eyes. "Makes more sense than the kitchen."

"I guess that's true."

She gave the addresses a quick check and tucked the stack back in the drawer. "Besides, they aren't hers. They're from someone named Connie to Davis."

Pax's hands froze while caressing hers. His whole body froze, from his facial muscles to his legs. "What did you just say?"

"Connie—"

"Let me see." Pax bent over and scooped the stack back up. "What's wrong?"

"That's my mother."

The information didn't fit with anything he had told her about the woman who gave birth to him. She had a breakdown and left. She'd died long ago without any word to her sons. "Really?"

He paged through each envelope, his gaze scanning each line of the address. With his finger, he tested the closures. "I don't get this."

"What do you mean?"

He shook his head as his voice became distant. "She never contacted us. She gave us up and that was it. No contact."

The evidence in his hands suggested otherwise. "It looks like she tried to write Davis but he never opened them. For some reason, Lara has the stack."

Pax sat down hard on the edge of the bed. He stared at the letters but his gaze didn't focus. It was as if he was looking into a window to another place.

She sat down next to him and rubbed her hand over his thigh. "Are you okay?"

"No. Davis never told me. Strike that, he actually lied to me and insisted our mother never checked in."

Kelsey's mind went to her own father and all the dysfunction that came with her early life and Pax's. "Davis probably thought knowing might hurt you. That you both needed to move on and the letters held you back."

At least she hoped that was true. In her mind there was no way listening to his birth mother excuse her behavior could be good for him. He overcame. He walked away and made a life separate from the horrors of what he'd seen. He didn't let his abandonment define him.

His strength and dignity in light of all he'd been through was part of what made him who he was. Part of what attracted her. No matter how she tried to pull away from him, to not care, watching him sucked her in.

She could love him without even trying. The idea his mother missed out on all that should have made Kelsey feel sorry for her, but all she could muster was hate.

Pax flipped the stack over and over. "That wasn't his choice."

And the brothers had to work that part out. There was likely some big-brother explanation, but that was for Davis to offer. "I agree, but from the dates you were in your late teens. I can imagine him wanting to protect you."

Pax's gaze flew to hers. "Why are you siding with him?"

"I don't even know him."

He threw the stack on the bed. "Which is my point."

The conversation had taken an odd turn, and she tried to pull it back. "I'm saying this is a piece of your past, something you need to discuss and deal with, but not something that matters in terms of who you are now. You've escaped whatever happened back then."

"I thought I had." He stood up and stalked to the door.

"Pax?"

He stopped but didn't turn around to face her. "I need to go out for a second."

"It's still not safe." She repeated the warning Connor issued many times before they left the office to come back here again.

"I need air." Then he was gone. His footsteps thudded on the steps. Even with the limp, it sounded as if he took them two at a time.

"Pax, wait!" She ran after him, but by the time she got to the top of the stairs she heard the front door slam.

She stood in the family room, stunned at the change in him. She spun around, trying to figure out what to do next. Her head spun and her mind raced. It took her a second to pick up on the muffled ringing of a phone. She searched the tables and couch. Saw Pax's phone sitting there, which meant he was even more vulnerable outside.

The sound finally led her to the bag under the coffee table. She unzipped it and reached inside.

Her phone. She'd forgotten Pax had grabbed it in her apartment. She'd missed the call but she punched a button to bring up the screen. Thirteen calls from one number. Her father's. She checked the text messages.

The last one came in ten minutes ago and was signed by her brother—Come Now.

Her brain rioted with the pros and cons of going. She tried to return the call but the phone just rang. They'd never been close, but that didn't mean she could abandon him. It took her another fifteen minutes to do a quick search for Pax outside. Not finding him and knowing he didn't have his cell, she grabbed his keys and texted Joel on the way out.

With any luck, Pax would come right behind her.

PAX KNEW SOMETHING was wrong the second he stepped back into Davis's house. The alarm was set but the house was deadly quiet. He called out for Kelsey but didn't get an answer.

He'd screwed up. His brain had turned to mush at seeing the letters…and he'd taken it out on her. But she had to be there. She knew the danger of roaming the streets. Hell, she'd warned him of just that when he stormed out.

Ready to take whatever anger she wanted to throw at him, he ran up the stairs. At first he walked from room to room. Then he raced. He threw open doors and closets as he screamed her name.

A mix of anger and dread pumped through him. He couldn't hear anything but the sound of the blood racing through his body. He reached for his phone on the corner of the coffee table just as it rang.

"What's going on?" Joel's voice sounded on the other end of the line.

The question sucked the rest of the life out of Pax. "What do you mean?"

"Kelsey texted about trouble and—"

Pax trampled right over the rest of Joel's sentence. "Where is she?"

Silence pounded for a few seconds before Joel answered. "She should be there. Wait, your car is moving."

"Track it."

"What are you going to do?"

Pax didn't even have to think about his response. He was in the kitchen digging through the utility drawer right now. "Borrow Davis's car and stop her."

Joel cleared his throat. "You mean follow her."

"No, I don't."

Chapter Eighteen

Kelsey's steps faltered as she walked up the stairs to the front door of her father's massive house. Not her house. Cold and sterile, it had never really been a home to her. She'd lived there and studied there. Gotten ignored there.

She preferred her cozy apartment and the man who'd left four screaming voice mails for her during the drive over to Virginia. Pax had been furious at first. Then he begged her to pull over.

She secretly hoped that meant something. Maybe he cared even a little, which would be convenient since she'd fallen stupid in love with him in a matter of days. Somewhere along the line she'd gone from the woman who doubted love to one who hoped it would happen to her. With Pax.

But she couldn't turn back or stop now. Not when Sean was in some sort of danger.

Pax had been right about that, too. She craved a connection of some kind with Sean. They'd never share memories from their childhood or hang out for fun, but her concern for him extended past a routine Christmas card at the holidays. Or it did now.

She reached the top step just as the door flew open. Her father stood there with a crazed look in his eyes and disheveled hair. She'd never seen the wild strain in him. He usually telegraphed control. That was one of his gifts. He could make everyone believe he was in command even as he scammed them out of their cash.

"It's about time you got here." He practically spit the words out at her.

No way was she going in there without Pax. It took all of her willpower just to drive into the state. "Where's Sean?"

Her father nodded behind him. "Inside."

Tension bounced off him and into her. "Tell him to come out."

"He's eating."

She remembered the panicked voice in the voice mails. The idea Sean left those and now sat somewhere eating crackers didn't fit together. She called out for him. "Sean, I'm here."

"Stop making all that noise."

She realized her father held one of his hands behind his back. The armband of his golf shirt was ripped and there was something on his pants. A dark stain.

Explanations bombarded her brain, each worse than the one before. "What did you do?"

"I've had enough of this." Her father let out a growl like that of a sick, wild beast.

With quickness she didn't expect, he reached out and grabbed her arm. His fingers dug into her flesh with a shocking toughness and he breathed heavily through his nose as he dragged her toward the door and entryway beyond.

She twisted and pounded a fist against his chest. Her hand caught against the doorway as she funneled her energy into staying on her feet and pulling away from him.

Then she saw the gun. He pointed it right at her head.

Father of the Year.

Her stomach flipped. Just to think she sat there and lectured Pax on family responsibility an hour ago when she came from this. A demented sense of loyalty combined with a total lack of conscience. That described her tainted family tree.

"You have two seconds to get in this house."

She swallowed back the bile rushing up her throat and shrugged out of his hold. With her head held high she walked back into the one place guaranteed to bring her to her emotional knees.

Turning a corner, she walked into her father's study and saw Sean tied to the chair. His head lolled to the side and blood dribbled from the corner of his mouth.

She fell to her knees and tried to rouse him. Fear pummeled her, threatening to swamp the last of her common sense. "Sean, no. Are you okay?"

"He's fine."

She spun around to face her father. He walked around, eyeing up his gun and acting as if nothing out of the ordinary was happening around him. "What is wrong with you?"

"Your brother lost his nerve. I blame all that babying from his mother."

The breath whooshed out of her and she sat back on her haunches to keep from falling over. "You? You're at the bottom of this Kingston thing."

He walked around to his desk and sat in his oversized leather chair. "Don't blame me. I was trying to help fix the mess Sean made."

She could see it all now. Sean made a decision and confided in their father. The old man saw dollar signs, as he always did, and the whole thing blew up. "By getting him to steal documents? He could be arrested."

"Pipe down. He did that on his own." Her father leaned back in his chair. "I stepped in when he lost his nerve to go through with the deal. He's already committed the act, so why not benefit? This is fixable so long as you brought the box he sent you."

Just like her father. This was one of his typical schemes. He saw an opportunity to rush in and steal money, and he did it.

She eyed up the gun in front of him on the desktop and judged the distance between her and the weapon and the chance of getting shot.

He laughed at her just as he'd done his whole life. "Don't even try it."

"Maybe she won't but I will." The male voice came from the hallway.

Kelsey had barely processed the mess in this room before she saw a new threat in the hall. The guy, so familiar but after her last few days her mind refused to work fast enough to place him. He stood there with a weapon of his own. Her breath caught in her throat.

Her father aimed his weapon as his eyes narrowed. "Who are you?"

"I'm afraid you're in the way." The younger man didn't hesitate. He raised the gun and fired. The shot had her father spinning as he dropped his weapon and reached for the red spot blooming on his shoulder.

"How dare you?"

Before her brain cleared, she reacted on instinct, leaping for her father's gun. The stranger caught her with a knee to the back and dropped her back to the floor. "Uh-uh. Don't go there."

She turned her head to the side. From this angle she couldn't look up, but the weight against her back eased. Slow and careful not to upset this guy, she sat up again. "Please let us go."

"I don't think so. See, now it's your turn."

The pieces finally clicked together in her head. She remembered the look on his face when he saw her. He went white and his eyes popped. Now she knew why. "You're the guy from the warehouse. Bryce Kingston's assistant."

"Glenn, and thank you for stopping by today. It allowed me to find you and follow you, especially after you took care of the decoy car." He reached down and lifted her with a hand under her armpit.

She couldn't figure out how much danger she was in. With her stomach rolling and her head in full-on dizziness mode, her body prepared for a fight-or-flight response. "I don't understand."

"I'm the one who paid your baby brother to grab the proprietary information. It should have been simple for a guy like him. Obtain it, hand it over then take the fall while I collected money from Kingston's competitor. It would have worked except he had an attack of guilt and wanted out. That sort of thing is not an option with the gentlemen we were dealing with."

Her father groaned and a kick of pity hit her out of nowhere. "Let me check my father."

Glenn pointed his gun at Sean's unconscious form. "I'd rather you untie your brother because it's time for him to play his final part in this."

"What if I don't?"

"I'll kill you first."

PAX HEARD THE THREAT and forced his legs to remain still. He made sure Connor and Joel heard the confession over the comm so they could tape it as they raced to the scene at the Virginia mansion. They needed to know what they were walking into. Someone had to report the truth.

Pax's inclination when he turned onto the street had been to race up the driveway and go in there and drag Kelsey home. He spied the car in front of him just in time. After parking down the block and dodging from overgrown bush to overgrown bush to hide, he came up the side of the house and listened from the hall.

Glenn Harber.

An assistant and totally off the radar. They'd been looking at Bryce, and he did have many sins on his scorecard and a huge amount of legal trouble ahead, but they all missed the easy answer. The guy with just as much access—possibly more—as his boss.

Connor had already reported on the questioning back at the warehouse. Dan was their inside man. He reported to the Pentagon crowd and got Corcoran hired for the protection job on Kelsey. Bryce thought he controlled everything, but he had no idea what was happening around him.

But the Glenn piece was a surprise.

Pax wanted to storm into the room, but Connor kept up a constant stream of conversation in his ear, advising on what to do and how to maintain control. With the tiny remote camera in his hand, Pax bent the thin wire and slipped the instrument around the corner.

As Pax watched, Kelsey untied her brother as he slowly came awake. But Glenn was in charge. He stood in front of them both with his back to Pax.

Pax could get off a shot but he risked Glenn getting off one of his own, and the chances of that target being Kelsey was too great to risk.

"Get up." Glenn motioned for Kelsey to help Sean to his feet.

"She's not involved in this." Doubled over and holding his stomach, Sean still managed to pivot so his body blocked Glenn's clean shot at Kelsey.

Pax hated the kid, planned to shake some sense into him, but the protective move saved him from getting punched. Glenn talked while Connor reported on his position. He was still ten minutes out, which meant this one was up to Pax.

"Since she's here, I'm thinking she knows something." Glenn shifted until his body was even with Kelsey's, and then he picked up her father's abandoned gun. "Do you have the stolen material, Ms. Moore?"

She shook her head. "The police have it."

Glenn laughed. "I doubt you'd risk your brother's freedom like that."

From this position, Pax had a wide view of her. He could see her hand tapping on the desk behind her. Her fingers searched, likely for a weapon. Much more of that and Glenn would put a bullet in her.

Glenn took a step toward Kelsey and Pax moved. He had the element of surprise on his side and didn't intend to waste it. Launching his body, he slammed into Glenn.

Wiry and smaller, the young man went flying into the bookcases. His footing fumbled but he held on to the gun. Only his aim changed, this time to point at Kelsey.

With the injury, Pax couldn't judge his steps. He tried to pivot from attacking Glenn to getting to Kelsey in time. Just as he pulled in close, she shoved him away, turning so that she'd take the brunt of any hit.

A shot boomed through the room as it exploded into chaos. Her father yelled and her brother took a step forward. Momentum carried Pax through the air.

To prevent a head-to-head shoot-out, Pax made a second move for Glenn, crashing into him and not caring if he blocked a bullet with his chest, if that meant keeping Kelsey safe. The air rushed out of the other man as they went rolling across the floor.

Glenn lifted an arm, but Pax proved faster. He also had the height and weight advantage, plus years of training. They smacked against the carpet, and Pax didn't wait. He straddled Glenn and punched the guy until blood poured from his nose and kept going until his eyes rolled back. Pax grabbed Glenn's gun before his head hit the floor.

Connor screamed for status and Pax managed one word. "Clear."

His only thought was for Kelsey. The shot still echoed in his brain and pain pounded into him at the thought of turning and seeing her injured. The idea of her body bloodied and broken drove him to his knees. When he spun around, he saw her on the floor with Sean's head on her lap.

Pax was on his knees and on top of them before she could say a word. "Were you hit?"

Tears rolled down her cheeks until she hiccupped and her chest heaved. "Sean."

Pax looked down. Blood and a pale face. The kid got clipped in the side. Probably not serious but he needed immediate attention and so did their father, who had passed out in his chair. "Connor, we need medical for the Moore men. Now."

"Kelsey?"

"She's fine." Still, Pax couldn't take in what he saw. His gaze skipped to Sean's glassy one. "You took a bullet for her."

Sean's eyes closed as his breathing grew heavy. "She was trying to protect you, so I protected her. I should have done it a long time ago."

The words opened the floodgates. Fury spilled through Pax. The danger, the risks. All the stupid decisions this kid had made and how he'd pulled Kelsey down with him.

Pax looked into the sweet eyes of the one woman who meant everything. Seeing the strain around her mouth and Sean's blood on her shirt set a torch to Pax's rage. "What were you thinking?"

Her head tipped back in shock. "I was trying to help you."

The fact she got defensive put him even further on the offensive. "You almost got killed."

She had the nerve to run a hand over his chin as a small smile inched over her lips. "I'm fine."

"I'm furious."

Her eyes narrowed as her hand dropped. "I can see that."

Part of him wanted to hold her, but he just kept yelling. He couldn't hold back even though the words sliced through them as they came out of his mouth. "I told you to stay at the house."

Her face closed up. "I didn't have that choice. And do not yell at me."

Pax stood up. He had to pace off some of the leftover energy coursing through him before he said something that hurt her. Having Connor and Joel shout warnings in his ear wasn't helping.

Pax didn't want to be tactful or understanding. But he needed to take all the rage of the past few hours over the attacks and the letters and funnel it somewhere.

Sean reached up to take her hand. "Who is this guy?"

She stared at Pax and he stared back. "My boyfriend."

Sean coughed until his body jackknifed. "Are you sure?"

Kelsey didn't bother to look up at Pax that time. "I guess not."

Chapter Nineteen

Kelsey wiped down the counter. The frantic scrubbing had her elbow aching, but she kept going even after Mike shot her a confused look and Lindy rolled her eyes in the you're-so-stupid way young women did.

After the days away and a round of fumigation and furious cleaning, it felt right to be back in the shop. She'd served about a thousand cups of coffee already today, or so it felt like. The unending line of chitchat from her regular customers started with questions about why they'd closed without notice and shifted to demands for reassurance that the shop would be open every day from now on.

It would because she had nothing else to do. The work kept her mind off Pax and her brain in motion. If she slowed down for even a second, his face popped into her mind and a hollow sensation rumbled in her stomach. Thinking about him led to missing him, and that brought on a stabbing pain around her heart.

Four days without him. Four days of looking up when the bell above the door dinged. And nothing.

His last words had been in anger. They still rang in her ears. He'd lectured her on safety, kissed her on the forehead as if she was a little kid and sent her on her way. It was insulting and hurtful. She wanted to kick him and punch him and make him apologize so they could get their relationship back on track.

With a crick in her neck and a sore lower back, she looked up from the lemon polish and gleaming glass countertop and scanned the shop. Seven tables filled and the laptop crowd lined up in front of Mike to grab black coffees and then claim the couches. It was a little after ten and everything appeared to be under control.

Everything except the shaking in her hands and heaviness weighing down her insides.

She tucked the rag into the waistband of her jeans and glanced at Mike. "I'm going to the back for a second."

The back. She hated that part of the shop now. The attackers that idiot Glenn from Kingston sent had seen to that.

When he'd signed up her brother for the moneymaking scheme, Glenn had set off a chain of events that had driven danger right to her. He'd stolen a piece of her security.

Thanks to his behavior, she was triple-checking locks and dealing with a high-end alarm system Connor had recommended and then sent a team to install. Not to be confused with the team he sent to rehab her apartment and the stairs.

At least someone at Corcoran cared about her. Shame it was the wrong guy.

She shoved open the swinging door to the office and came to a stop on the other side. She heard the whomp of the door behind her as it closed, but all she cared about was the guy in front of her.

She blinked and then blinked again, but he didn't disappear. "Pax?"

He stood halfway down the hall with his hands in the front pockets of his jeans and a polo shirt stretching across his broad chest. "You used the same code for the back door as you had on your old system. You need to change it."

Fury reached up and slapped her. She'd been missing him,

trying not to love him, and here he was acting like the big-time security dude rather than like the guy who owed her a huge explanation. "You're supposed to come in the front door."

"I was avoiding the crowd."

For some reason the flat tone and way he rocked back on his heels ticked her off even more. "You can't be back here. Go out front."

She reached for her office door and missed the knob. The shaking in her hand and blurring of her vision made her big exit impossible.

"Kelsey."

She crowded the door and fumbled to get it open and sneak inside. "Go away."

"Stop." He slipped in behind her with his body pressing against hers.

Heat seeped into her frozen limbs from his chest, and the seductive pull of his scent wound around her. Much more of the closeness and touching and her head would explode. But she refused to turn around or lean back and accept his comfort.

She needed him to leave. After everything they'd been through and how he left it, there was no way she was going to break down in front of him.

His hands braced on the wall on each side of her head. A tremble raced down her spine when his lips brushed against her hair. "You should go."

"Not until we talk."

She ignored the dull rumble of the crowd on the other side of the door and pulled in energy from every limb and turned around. The shove against his muscled chest came next, but he didn't budge. "Now you want to chat? You ran out—"

"I didn't."

"—and didn't bother to call, and now you want attention?

Well, no thank you. I've had enough of that kind of behavior from my father. I don't need it from you, too."

"Please don't compare me to him. Watching him pull a gun on you… Just don't."

If Pax hadn't used the plea or didn't seem so flat and sad, she may have kept the shield up. But seeing the lines around his mouth and stress tugging on his face chipped away at her control.

She'd spent nights alone and awake. A glance in the mirror just that morning told her she resembled the step before death. The pain in his eyes struck her as painfully familiar.

"Where have you been?" The words came out before she could stop them. She meant to push him away and tell him she didn't care…but she did.

He leaned in until his face hovered a foot away from hers. "I went to Hawaii. Took a red-eye back."

Her head pushed back into the door. Of all the responses she anticipated, that one was not on the list. "What?"

"I had to see Davis about the letters, get him to explain them." Pax spread his hand at the base of her neck and rubbed his thumb over her collarbone.

The soft touch had her traitorous nerve endings tingling. "But he's on his honeymoon."

"Believe it or not, he took it well. Better than he accepted the news about the operation and Kingston. It was pretty clear he thought I should be recuperating."

She'd never met Davis and already liked him. He seemed to have gotten the common sense in the Weeks family. "He's not alone in that feeling."

Pax's mouth didn't lift. The flat line drew all of his features down. "I wanted to confront the past then let it go. Deal with it and walk away."

She'd said something similar to him days ago and he'd shrugged it off. "Did you get what you needed?"

"In part." His fingertips drew lazy circles over her skin. "See, I've spent so many years hating my mother. At least that's what was on the surface. Underneath I think I wanted, just once, to hear from her. To know she cared or that she regretted leaving us behind."

Kelsey's heart shredded for the scared boy he was and the conflicted man he'd grown up to be. "That makes you human, Pax."

"I guess."

"And the letters gave you the answers?" She asked the question but refused to let hope take hold. Even if he found what he needed that didn't mean he was ready to move forward or truly could.

"I don't know, since I haven't read them. Davis hasn't either and Lara gets so furious with her desire to kick my now-dead mother's butt that she can't look, either. Davis insists it's how he wants it. Ignoring them but keeping them around works for him. His way of getting over the past was to decide the contents of the letters didn't matter."

Having lived with a father's disdain, Kelsey struggled every day. Part of her believed not knowing him might have been better. Maybe now that Pax had worked so hard to overcome his rough childhood and desperate circumstances, his mother shouldn't get to cash in and be a part of his healthy present. She didn't deserve it.

"Do you agree with Davis's theory?"

"I'm still working that out, but I've accomplished most of what I wanted to do in talking it through with Davis. I get where he was coming from." Pax's hand moved up to her cheek. "I've stopped being angry about everything that came before."

"I'm happy for you." Her fingers dug into his forearms as a rush of light poured through her. The crowd noise blended into the background and the normal creaking sounds from the old row house fell away.

"It's all because of you. What's good and right and what's working. You and the team own that."

Her breath hiccupped and her leg muscles threatened to give way. "I didn't—"

"When a man meets the woman he wants to walk into the future next to, he figures out how to let go of the past." His gaze searched her face, landing on her lips and then traveling back to her eyes as the seconds ticked by. "Say something."

Joy bubbled right under the surface. She tried to stomp it back down. Not let it take hold. That way invited pain, and after days of it she wasn't sure she could handle much more. "I'm afraid to."

"Then I'll keep going." Both hands framed her face and his eyes glittered. "I care for you Kelsey Moore. Someday real soon I'm going to use the word *love,* because that's what it is. Weird, I know, since it's been such a short time. But this relationship has been in fast-forward from the start, and I don't want to put on the brakes."

Her body went still. She couldn't hear anything but his deep, soothing voice and the frantic beat of her own heart. "Love."

"I don't want to scare you."

She closed her eyes and let a mix of relief and excitement wash over her. Hope turned to happiness, and her head sang at his words.

She pressed closer to him as her hands toured up his muscled arms to his chest. "Losing you scares me. Loving you is easy."

"You're saying *love?*"

It was a challenge and she accepted it with relish. "Yes… well, soon."

His forehead tapped against hers, and his hands slipped

into her hair. "Please forgive me for walking out. I couldn't hear your voice while I was gone because I knew I'd come rushing back to be with you. All that anger and confusion over my mother and over Davis's choices hit me out of nowhere, and I have to work it out."

The explanation was simple and sweet, and every ounce of hurt dripped away. With her hands under his chin, she lifted his head and stared into those eyes that made her heart skip. "You can't do it alone."

"I don't want to." His lips touched against hers, quick and sure.

She wanted so much more. "I'm serious, Pax. Next time, whether it's personal or work, you need to let me in. Don't push me away. And you sure better not hop on a plane and leave."

He held her hand against his chest and his gaze remained serious. "Being without you for four days nearly broke me."

She couldn't hold the smile back one more second. "That's better."

"You want me to beg? Because I will."

She threw her arms around his neck and stretched up on tiptoes. "I want you to come upstairs and tell me all about this loving and caring, and then I can tell you how I feel the same way."

She kissed him then. Not sweet and not short. Long and loving, letting him know the heartache she experienced being alone and her desperate plea that it never happen again.

When they came up for air, that sexy grin was in place on his mouth. "Why, Ms. Moore, are you seducing me in the middle of the morning?"

"Would you rather have a doughnut?" Right now she'd give him anything.

Sometime, after the punch of excitement died down and

a few weeks had passed, she'd offer him a place to stay. With her.

"You had me the minute you walked in here with that beaten-down expression and offered to beg." Before that, actually, but he'd get the idea.

And she knew he did when he picked her up. She wrapped her legs around his lean hips and leaned back against the door.

"That did it for you, huh?"

Everything about him worked for her. "Always."

He let her legs drop and treated her to a wink. "Then let's get out there and serve some coffee."

"I offered to seduce you."

"Oh, we'll get to that but you have a business to run. I can respect that, and I can help."

"You're going to work here today?" She thought of him in an apron with a gun and burst out laughing.

"I'm going to watch you and plan some bedroom activities for the end of the workday. Think of it as multitasking."

She kissed him one last time and then slipped past him. After two steps, she smiled at him over her shoulder. "Are you ready?"

"For you? Definitely."

* * * * *

REQUEST YOUR FREE BOOKS!
2 FREE NOVELS PLUS 2 FREE GIFTS!

H HARLEQUIN®

INTRIGUE®

BREATHTAKING ROMANTIC SUSPENSE

YES! Please send me 2 FREE Harlequin Intrigue® novels and my 2 FREE gifts (gifts are worth about $10). After receiving them, if I don't wish to receive any more books, I can return the shipping statement marked "cancel." If I don't cancel, I will receive 6 brand-new novels every month and be billed just $4.74 per book in the U.S. or $5.24 per book in Canada. That's a savings of at least 14% off the cover price! It's quite a bargain! Shipping and handling is just 50¢ per book in the U.S. and 75¢ per book in Canada.* I understand that accepting the 2 free books and gifts places me under no obligation to buy anything. I can always return a shipment and cancel at any time. Even if I never buy another book, the two free books and gifts are mine to keep forever.

182/382 HDN F42N

_____
Name   (PLEASE PRINT)

_____
Address   Apt. #

_____
City   State/Prov.   Zip/Postal Code

_____
Signature (if under 18, a parent or guardian must sign)

Mail to the **Harlequin® Reader Service:**
IN U.S.A.: P.O. Box 1867, Buffalo, NY 14240-1867
IN CANADA: P.O. Box 609, Fort Erie, Ontario L2A 5X3

**Are you a subscriber to Harlequin Intrigue books
and want to receive the larger-print edition?
Call 1-800-873-8635 or visit www.ReaderService.com.**

* Terms and prices subject to change without notice. Prices do not include applicable taxes. Sales tax applicable in N.Y. Canadian residents will be charged applicable taxes. Offer not valid in Quebec. This offer is limited to one order per household. Not valid for current subscribers to Harlequin Intrigue books. All orders subject to credit approval. Credit or debit balances in a customer's account(s) may be offset by any other outstanding balance owed by or to the customer. Please allow 4 to 6 weeks for delivery. Offer available while quantities last.

Your Privacy—The Harlequin® Reader Service is committed to protecting your privacy. Our Privacy Policy is available online at www.ReaderService.com or upon request from the Harlequin Reader Service.

We make a portion of our mailing list available to reputable third parties that offer products we believe may interest you. If you prefer that we not exchange your name with third parties, or if you wish to clarify or modify your communication preferences, please visit us at www.ReaderService.com/consumerchoice or write to us at Harlequin Reader Service Preference Service, P.O. Box 9062, Buffalo, NY 14269. Include your complete name and address.

HI13R

SPECIAL EXCERPT FROM

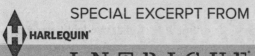

HARLEQUIN®

INTRIGUE®

Read on for a sneak-peek of USA TODAY *bestselling author Debra Webb's first installment of her brand-new* COLBY AGENCY: THE SPECIALISTS *series,*

Bridal Armor

At the airport in Denver, Colby Agency spy Thomas Casey is intercepted by the only woman who ever made him think twice about his unflinching determination to remain unattached…

She flashed an overly bright smile and handed him a passport. "That's you, right?"

He opened it and, startled, gazed up at her. "Who are you?"

"You know me," she murmured, leaning closer. "Thomas."

His eyes went wide as he recognized her voice under the disguise.

"I need you." The words were out, full of more truth than she cared to admit regarding their past, present and, quite possibly, their immediate future.

He nodded once, all business, and fell in beside her as she headed toward an employee access. She refused to look back, though she could feel Grant closing in as the door locked behind them.

"This way."

"Tell me what's going on, Jo."

She ignored the ripple of awareness that followed his using her given name. It wasn't the reaction she'd expected. Thomas always treated everyone with efficient professionalism. Except for that one notable, extremely personal, incident years ago.

"I'll tell you everything just as soon as we're out of here." She checked her watch. They had less than five minutes before the cabbie she'd paid to wait left in search of another fare. "Keep up. We have to get out of the area before the roads are closed." She'd taken precautions, given herself options, but no one could prepare for a freak blizzard.

"Are you in trouble?"

"Yes." On one too many levels, she realized. But it was too late to back out now. If she didn't follow through, someone more objective would take over the investigation. Based on what she'd seen, she didn't think that was a good idea.

Moving forward, she hoped some deep-seated instinct would kick in, making him curious enough to cooperate with her.

"Jo, wait."

Would the day ever come when his voice didn't create that shiver of anticipation? "No time."

"I need an explanation."

"And I'll give you one when we're away from the airport."

Can Jo be trusted or is it a trap?
Then again, nothing is too dangerous for these agents...
except falling in love.

Don't miss
Bridal Armor
by Debra Webb

Book one in the
COLBY AGENCY: THE SPECIALISTS SERIES

Available August 20, edge-of-your-seat romance,
only from Harlequin® Intrigue®!

HIEXP0913

SADDLE UP AND READ 'EM!

Looking for another great Western read? Check out these September reads from the SUSPENSE category!

COWBOY REDEMPTION by Elle James
Covert Cowboys
Harlequin Intrigue

MOST ELIGIBLE SPY by Dana Marton
HQ: Texas
Harlequin Intrigue

Look for these great Western reads and more available wherever books are sold or visit
www.Harlequin.com/Westerns

INTRIGUE®

INTRIGUE

*HE WAS ASSIGNED TO PROTECT HER...
NOT MAKE HER HIS OWN.*

Cale Lane had his orders: keep Cassidy Sherridan alive at all costs. But who sent six armed men storming the Rio ballroom to take her out? The gorgeous party girl wasn't giving it up. Now he had a more urgent mission: uncover Cassidy's secrets...one by one.

GLITTER AND GUNFIRE

BY *USA TODAY* BESTSELLING AUTHOR

CYNTHIA EDEN
PART OF THE SHADOW AGENTS SERIES.

*Catch the thrill August 20,
only from Harlequin® Intrigue®.*

HI69712